SINSTER

SHORTS

First published in Great Britain by Wide Awake Books 2022

ISBN: 978-1-9162985-5-2

A CIP catalogue record for this book is available from the British Library.

SINISTER

SHORTS

By Adam D. Searle

Illustrated by Janine Van Moosel

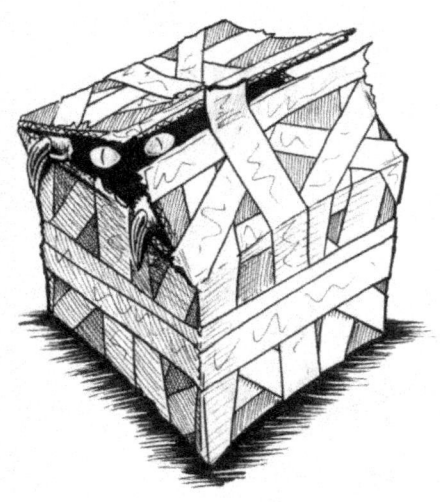

CONTENTS

BEHIND THE GARAGE DOOR

There was something strange going on in the garage.

Both twins knew something was not right, but their parents didn't believe them.

The twins first heard the noise not too long after moving into their new house nine months ago.

At first it started as a shuffling sound, as if something was crawling or sliding across the concrete floor from inside.

The garage sat slumped against the side of their tall house, surrounded by a towering brick wall where the tops of the trees peered over. There was no access to the garage from inside of the house, only a metal door which had to be lifted at the front, and a heavy, wooden door at the back. So, the twins knew that nobody was inside of the garage at the time.

"It could be a rat," their father suggested that evening after Terri had recounted the story to her mum and dad. "Maybe it's best you both stayed out."

It was not as if Terri or her brother Jack ever ventured out into the garage anyway. They never did at their old house, and would not do here either. They were nine years old, and had a narrow but long garden to play in with trees and bushes, and a shed where their bikes and games were stored. Their dad enjoyed woodwork while their mum liked to paint, so the garage was their shared workshop and studio.

1

One weekend, soon afterwards, the twins had gone outside to play and that was when Terri heard the sound once again.

"Dad said it was a rat!" Jack told her rather crossly when she pulled him over to listen. They both leaned against the thick door, their ears pressed against the wood. Due to the surrounding wall and trees, the passageway which led through from the back garden to the garage was always in the shade, no matter what time of the year it was, and Terri felt a shiver of cold run down her spine.

From inside the empty garage there was only silence.

And just when Jack looked as if he was going to push himself away from the door, the sound came again, this time a frantic shuffling as something hurried towards the door. Terri gasped, her heart thundering in her chest.

It was not a rat — it sounded bigger.

Jack pressed his ear firmly to the door, his eyes wide.

The noise stopped suddenly at the door, and Terri felt her breath catch in her throat. A growl came, full of menace and anger much like an aggressive dog, snarling from inside. The twins leapt back just as something heavy and forceful banged against the door and they both screamed.

*

It was after school on a heavy and sweltering hot day.

Terri, as silently as she could, reached up for where the keys, in all shapes and sizes, hung from a peg, and grasped the long key that sat on the hook by itself. The keys jingled loudly, and Terri froze for just a second, before continuing. Then she unhooked it and pulled it down and slipped it inside of her shirt before turning to the kitchen. Inside her mum had her back to her as she stood at the cooker throwing sliced vegetables into a large pan which was boiling noisily away.

Terri hurried into the living room and over to Jack, who was sitting on the sofa with his cap on his head. He was so engrossed in his mobile that he took no notice of her until she punched him on the arm.

"Ow!"

"Shoosh!" she hushed him; finger pressed to her lips. "Come on," she nodded with her head to the back door, and Jack groaned as he threw his mobile aside. Terri reached down and grasped his arm and pulled him to his feet.

Barefooted, the twins hurried out into the sun-drenched garden where the table and chairs sat by a waiting barbeque, which their father would light up later when he came home from work.

The twins hurried around the side of the house, where the dark, cool shadows swallowed them up. They came to the garage and pressed their ears to the door, but they heard no sounds over their own heavy breathing.

"You sure you want to do this?" Jack asked, raising his eyebrows.

"Yes, we both agreed," she replied as they stepped away from the door. Terri took the key out from inside her shirt.

Since hearing the growl a few months back, the twins had heard noises a number of times. During the weekends, when their parents had been working in the garage or out in the front in the driveway, the twins had wandered around inside but had seen no sign of anything that could make such a noise.

There was a workbench against the wall beside the back door, a few cardboard boxes that were full of items that had not yet been unpacked, some toolboxes and a load of wood. But there was also a funny smell… lingering beneath the scent of paints, oils and saw dust. A horrid smell that was kind of like rotting meat. Their parents did not like them going into the garage due to the tools and equipment their father had there for

3

his woodwork, so their complaints were often overlooked by the adults.

Trying to keep her hand steady, Terri inserted the key into the lock and twisted, and the lock clicked loudly as the bolt was pulled back home. She grabbed the large black doorknob, which felt as cold as ice in her hand.

"You really sure about this?" Jack asked nervously, fanning his face with his hat. "Why don't we go around the front instead?"

"Because mum would hear," she told her brother. The front door of the garage always rattled loudly whenever it was opened.

Terri twisted the doorknob and pulled the heavy door open, and thick hot air burst over them and Jack staggered back and waved a hand in front of his face.

It was that smell again. Only stronger.

Terri stepped into the garage; her eyes wide as she looked around. Behind her, Jack followed as they slowly moved into the dark space.

Above their heads, wooden rafters crossed the ceiling. Thick coils of ropes hung from them swaying. Jack's foot kicked an empty food can, which clattered across the floor, startling both of them.

As they walked slowly and quietly into the middle of the garage, they noticed that the floor was littered with the empty, dented tins of cat and dog food. It was so hot that Terri felt her shirt sticking to her back, and the place stank so strong that she began to feel ill.

"Switch on the light," she ordered, her voice low. Jack grunted with protest and turned towards the back and suddenly froze.

Sensing her brother's sudden gasp, Terri turned and they both saw, from deep in the corner of the garage from under the

4

workbench that something had started to swarm from among the shadows.

Terri felt her breath catch in her throat; she took a step back. Jack remained where he was, wide-eyed and mouth open as something large started to crawl out.

A huge creature rose up so high that its head was inches from the rafters, its glowing eyes stared down at the two children, its mouth opened in a hiss.

"Get out," Terri urged, her voice filled with terror, but before she or her brother could move, one of the creature's many limbs reached out and towards the screaming twins.

*

The water was boiling nicely.

Inside the vast, deep pot, the vegetables swam and stirred among the bubbles.

She licked her lips as she added salt and then a sprinkle of pepper. She glanced over at the clock. Her husband would be home soon and then he would be on barbeque duty and he would have to get some meat. Her stomach growled hungrily.

She wondered where the twins were and hoped they were behaving. Most likely they were outside in the back garden.

She grabbed her slotted spoon and started to stir the vegetables, making sure she did not overboil the carrots.

She heard a noise from behind, something shuffling into the kitchen, stopping just inside the doorway.

"I hope you've both been good," she said, as she pulled a carrot out and tested it. Still firm, so she put it back in the water.

"Dinner won't be long now," she said, turning towards the doorway. "Your daddy will be home s…"

She froze, the spoon fell from her hand and clattered to the floor.

5

The twins stood side by side before her, splattered with blood. Jack's cap was missing and his hair was a mess, his vest hung in tatters from the one shoulder and one jean leg was torn up as far as the knee. Terri's shirt hung from her in rags, her shorts were ripped and torn, her knees were grazed and bleeding.

"Kids!"

Jack and Terri smiled, their lips pulling back to expose their razor-sharp pointed teeth. Teeth which stretched from ear to ear.

Their mother also smiled, revealing her own teeth, teeth which they hid while out amongst others who were not their kind.

Terri held out her hands, holding a lump of dripping dark meat. Their mother took the offering, her smile widening and saliva drippling down her chin as she turned to the cooker and placed it carefully into the pot of boiling water before turning back to her children.

She dropped to her knees and held out her arms and the twins ran to her and they embraced. She felt their claws growing from their fingers, the lumps of their spines, like triangles running down their backs. The smell of the sticky blood sharpening their senses and unleashing their true selves.

She had longed for the day when they could hunt and feast as a family.

THE END

THE LAUNDRY MONSTER

I am unsure exactly where it came from or how.

Or even when it suddenly turned up like it did.

But it was at least three or four weeks after mum had left that my two little brothers, Rick and Teddy, had finally convinced me about the monster in our house.

And that was the day it ate Teddy.

My name is Natalie and I am ten years old. Rick is seven and Teddy is four. We live in the last small house on the end of a quiet street across from the park. Dad was a mechanic who worked part time while mum worked nights at a supermarket, before she moved up north to do training.

When mum left, dad did not really cope all that well, and the first few days he did struggle to keep the household running.

I suppose it was down to me being the eldest to help out, but I am just a kid! A tomboy who never really took to household chores, and who never really minded living in a bit of a muddle anyway.

The house fell into a mess. Dust settled into clumps, toys were never tidied up and rubbish never emptied. Dirty plates and cutlery piled up in the sink and, pretty soon, the cupboards were bare and we had to wash what we needed. The cooker went unused, as our food came in the form of supermarket ready meals that we heated up in the microwave and often ate on our laps while watching tv.

The washing machine was another appliance that became redundant. Dad tried once, but ended up flooding the floor! So, clothes went unwashed and ended up piling up in the laundry basket in the upstairs cupboard, or all over our bedroom floors.

I did do my best in helping out. I made sure that my brothers were up and ready for school and had proper lunches and their school uniforms was as clean as possible. And I was thankful when the summer finally rolled in and the schools broke up.

Between the time I spent playing with my friends and making sure that my brothers (and dad) had something to eat, I never really took much notice of the pile of laundry as it grew bigger and bigger. And, as it was summer, clothing was not really something we needed much of, as we were living in our shorts and vests most of the days anyway.

Then, one morning, four weeks after mum had left, I was in my bedroom getting ready to go out to meet up with some friends for a game of footie. I was hunting around my bedroom searching for one of my football shirts (one which looked the cleanest) when I heard a thumping noise through the wall.

The boys shared the bedroom next to mine and I presumed that the sound was coming from them.

"What are you two up to?" I challenged as the noises persisted. I was getting annoyed; I couldn't find any of my Arsenal FC shirts, and I wondered if dad had been taking the dirty laundry out that I had thrown over my floor over the last few weeks.

"Not us," Rick piped up.

Both boys were sitting in the mess of their bedroom floor, bedcovers hanging from the side of their bunkbeds, toy boxes overturned, empty draws hanging open. Teddy had chocolate smeared around his mouth and on his T-shirt. I noticed that there was not a single item of dirty clothing on their floor either!

"It's the monster," Teddy whispered, as if afraid of being overheard.

I rolled my eyes and groaned in irritation. This monster business had started up the week before when both boys were convinced that there was a monster in our landing cupboard. I guess they came up with the idea after watching some video on the computer or something.

"There is no…" and that was as far as I got when something thumped on the wall. It was coming from the cupboard.

At first, we were all silent. Then I turned and left the room and headed out onto the landing and towards the cupboard. Musty sunlight filtered through from the small window and bleached the landing floor where some of Teddy's building blocks lay scattered. The boys followed me out, eyes wide and hair a mess.

"Don't open it!" Rick shouted; his voice edged with panic. I never heard him sounding so afraid before.

"Don't be daft," I told him reaching out and grasping the handle. The boys stood and watched as I yanked the door open. The laundry basket was so full that the clothing was piled high over the top. Shirts, shorts, jeans, towels…it stank.

"Ah-ha!"

And amongst the pile was one of my football shirts! I might be a tomboy, but I really didn't want to go out in my vest for a second day running! It already had grass stains down the front from the wrestling with my friends the day before. So, I reached out and grasped my shirt but, before I could pull it free the mound of laundry shifted and fell over my hand. I felt it tighten and then pull, not forcefully, but firmly — as if wanting to suck me in.

I frowned and tugged, but the clothing seemed to hold me in its grasp and I felt it tightening around my wrist. Panic flared in my chest as I pulled and tugged frantically at my trapped arm, aware how the pile of laundry had started to rise out of the basket like a pan of milk curdling, growing tall as it oozed up, towering higher and higher.

I screamed and gave a firm tug and my hand shot free. I staggered back and watched in wide-eyed terror as the basket toppled and fell, spilling the shifting mass of laundry over the floor by my feet. I staggered back and tumbled, landing with a painful bang on my backside. And all the while I watched as the mass of spilled laundry gathered up into a large wide blob which shifted and shook as it piled higher.

"Natalie!" My brothers ran over and I felt Rick's hand under my arms, pulling me up, but I just could not tear my eyes of from the monster created by our very own clothing. It uttered a groan as its huge mouth opened and I saw that my football shirt was now its tongue. Two small holes for its drooping eyes stared back.

"You see!" Rick snapped as he helped me to my feet.

"You see, Natalie!" Teddy repeated, turning to me, his chubby, food smeared face set firm. He pointed at the monster, which shuffled slowly closer to where we stood.

"Teddy…" I was going to tell him to keep away. I was going to reach out and pull him to me and hold him firmly and protect him, just like how a big sister should.

But a tentacle made from a leg of a pair of dad's jeans snatched out at him. It wrapped around Teddy's waist and I saw his face fall in terror for that brief second before he was suddenly whipped away with a cry.

"No!" Rick screamed as we watched our brother thrown into the monster's wide mouth which quickly closed down over him.

My heart sank and I dropped to my knees, shocked and defeated, feeling powerless watching as the monster's mouth went up and down, as if my brother was no more than a chunk of toffee or a piece of gum. Munching away as it sat piled on the

11

landing floor, wobbling in satisfaction with the meal it had taken.

My brother.

My sweet little brother.

He was only four years old.

And just as the first of my tears started to swell in my eyes, the monster spat him out.

Teddy, his eyes wide and mouth pulled back in a huge grin, flew out as naked as the day he had been born, and I caught him in my arms as he crashed into my chest with a force which sent me sprawling down on my back with my brother on top of me.

"That was fun!" Teddy declared, happily peering down at my face, his hair was a mess, but the food that had been smeared around his mouth seconds before was now gone.

"Again! Again!" Teddy declared jolting up and down on top of me like a child who wanted to go on a funfair ride.

"Let's get out of here!" Rick cried, and I did not need to be told twice.

*

A couple of days later we heard from mum, who reported happily that she would be coming home in the next few days.

Now, that sent us all into a panic, and Dad gave us our orders — we were going to have to work hard getting the house tidied up.

The last few days we were trying to deal with the monster. At first dad was like me and dismissed it, and it took a great effort to get him up the stairs to see it. And even then, it was only after he had been sucked in, eaten and spat back out again, that he finally believed us.

Together we managed to force it into the boy's bedroom and during that time Rick got eaten twice and Teddy a further three times! I had no intention of letting that smelly thing eat me, no matter how much fun my brothers claimed it was.

The monster resided in the room for a day before escaping out of the window. I'm not sure where it has gone, but based on the screams coming from the house at the back of ours, I can only guess.

I am sure mum will return to a clean and tidy house, although I don't know how we are going to explain what has happened to most of our clothes.

THE END

CHILDISH THINGS

And he was at it again!

On his computer with those funny headphones of his, the ones with that thin microphone; tapping away at his remote control, talking and swearing and cursing at whoever he was playing with. The screen before him ablaze with the flickering flashes of gunfire and explosions.

She did not dare to ask if he wanted to play with her, or even to spend at least a small bit of time with her, his only sister. She could tell from that angry look on his face that whatever game he was playing, he was losing.

Phoebe longed to spend time with her big brother, to play games or sit out in the garden together, where he used to entertain her with made-up stories. Sure, like all siblings, they hadn't always seen eye to eye and fights and arguments were common, but they were close and always found forgiveness and eventually made peace afterwards.

But since William had turned eleven and started his new school, he had become very irritable, angry and aggressive. He found himself a new group of friends and they were always either holed up in his bedroom playing computer games or were out somewhere until late, which worried their poor mum. Their mum was still not at all pleased that the police had bought William home one night not too long ago.

She missed her brother and longed to tell him about things she had discovered or had happened. Like how her friend Diane had fallen off her bike and had to have stitches in her knees, or the cool new trick she could do with her drawings.

She had tried a few times before, once even holding a page out in front of his face, but he'd just snatched it out of her hands and torn it up and told her to get lost.

She realised he did not care if he hurt her feelings or if she cried.

"Will, do you want to see my new picture?" she finally asked, going over to where he sat slouched in his chair. His face was as red as his T-shirt and his eyes were aglow with the flickering and flashing of the screen.

"No. I have not got time for your stupid, childish things," he shouted, his voice raw with anger.

She flinched and took a step back, clutching her picture to her chest. He did not even tear his eyes away from his game.

"Get the Hell out of my room and get out of my life."

She turned and sadly walked out as he cursed and swore as he hammered on his game console.

She made her way downstairs and out into the garden, where the spring sunshine greeted her. She walked over to the blanket laid out across the lawn under the tree where, once, William had entertained her with stories of magic and adventure. She had asked him if magic was real and she remembered that, quiet seriously, he had looked at her with his kind, blue eyes and told her, "Yes, if you truly believe it."

She lay down on the blanket where her giant notepad and crayons waited for her along with a pile of her drawings and she gently laid the one she had taken to show Will on top. Phoebe opened the notepad to a new page and picked up a red crayon.

The garden was alive with the sound of birdsong; daisies speckled the grass and bees flew from flower to flower. She hummed gently as she drew a new picture, a sea of green grass speckled with oversized daisies with overlapping petals; a blue sky with a round sun and a tree with bunches of leaves.

And, under the tree stood William in his red T-shirt, ripped jeans and messy long hair.

She had drawn a wide, happy smile on his face and, satisfied; Phoebe glanced away at her coloured crayons and found her blue. When she turned back to her picture, she saw that Williams smile had turned down into a frown. His stick arms were held up as if in horror and he had moved to stand in front of the tree. She suspected that up in his bedroom William's game continued to flash, while his headphones rested in his now empty chair.

"Never mind, Will," she told her brother. "I will draw you a football and some toys."

And she started work on a ball for her brother to play with. She never saw her pictures move as they only did that when she was not looking, but at least she would get time to play with her brother again.

THE END

THE GHOUL

Dean and Jasmine were horrified to learn of the recent activity at Seven Edges Cemetery.

The graveyard was old and rather massive, the grounds spreading and dipping and rising so you couldn't see from one end to the other. A high stone wall, green with moss and covered in places with tangles of ivy, surrounded the grounds with tall iron barred gates leading out at different points.

A wide gravel path led through the cemetery from one side to the other and this was where many people – mostly children – went through on their way to and from school. Gravestones of all sizes and styles stood erect, although many had fallen or toppled over through the decades. Trees and bushes sprouted up everywhere, and stone statues stood green with age.

That afternoon, as the warm sun filtered down and the air was alive with the sound of bird song and the distant drum of traffic, a group of children on their way home stood idly around in the middle of the wide gravel path at the place where it forked in two. The young group were deep in discussion expressing their concerns.

"It happened last night," whimpered one little boy, shivering.

"Yes, my father told me," a girl said, rather too excitedly. "Someone reported holes appearing in some of the graves."

"Yeah, and someone smashed the vase on my grandmother's grave," sniffed another boy.

Dean and Jasmine stood amidst the group as the others told what they had heard. They were all scared, Dean could hear that in their voices and his fist clenched tightly at his side.

Finally, the school friends decided to head home and with bids of goodbyes, they departed along the paths, their feet shuffling on the gravel as they went.

But Dean and Jasmine remained where they were, watching as the children walked away. The cemetery was not as busy as it usually was, a man on a bike raced passed them, his wheels spraying gravel as he went. In the distance, a dog barked at them as the woman tried to pull it along.

"Who could do something so horrible?" Jasmine asked sadly, turning to Dean.

"I don't know," he replied, anger in his voice. "But I sure intend to find out."

And Jasmine saw in his eyes that he meant it too.

*

Night fell heavily and cloaked the cemetery in darkness; in the trees and bushes the birds went silent, even the mice seemed weary as they scurried about.

Aided by the light of the moon which peered out from the clouds, Dean and Jasmine met in the middle of the graveyard where the gravel pathway parted and where the children had grouped earlier that day.

Silently, they moved through the cemetery. They passed drooping trees and went over old graves; many were overgrown and some held flowers that had long since dried up.

"The cemetery's so big, how are we going to find who is responsible?" Jasmine asked as they clambered over a fallen tree.

"I am not too sure," Dean replied. "But let's start at the north side, that was where the vandalism happened."

They made their way there and started looking for something that might help them identify who, or what, had caused the damage. After a while, just when they started to grow bored and tired of their hunt, they heard a noise. An evil chuckling of something laughing to themselves, something so sinister that even they were creeped out.

They followed the noise around a holly bush and there, amongst the tall grass, a figure hunched at an old grave, clawing away and flinging clumps of dirt behind it.

"Who are you? And what are you doing?" Jasmine asked sharply, more in shock than fear and horror. The figure froze, then turned to stare at the two children.

Their eyes went wide at what it was. Not a man or child as they had first thought but, instead, a horrid little creature with a hunched back and long arms.

It was a ghoul.

"What are you children doing here?" The ghoul demanded rather angrily; a string of saliva dangling from the corner of its sneering mouth. Its skin was grey and grubby with dirt, a charm made from bone hung from around of its scrawny neck. "You should not be here! This is my cemetery. All mine."

"No, it is not!" Dean finally found his voice and took a step towards the creature. Jasmine clutched at his arm.

"This cemetery is for everyone and you have no business doing what you have been doing. Begone with you."

But the ghoul just threw back its head and laughed wickedly up at the night sky, its teeth as square and as crooked as some of the gravestones in the cemetery itself.

"Please, everybody crosses the cemetery to get to school. If you continue doing what you do, they will stop," Jasmine said, pleading with the creature.

But the ghoul did not care.

"Leave me be or I will eat you both alive!" it roared in rage, its dark eyes lightening up with evil glare. Moonlight threw the shadow of its long arms across the ground towards them and Jasmine and Dean turned and fled, but Dean's final words were heard by the roaring ghoul:

"If you are not gone by tomorrow, you will be sorry."

*

The next day signs hung up on the cemetery gates informing the public about the criminal activity taking place at night.

Dean and Jasmine went with the children to school and back again. Many were concerned and a few had decided to go

21

the long way home instead of taking the shortcut across the cemetery.

Dean and Jasmine's anger burned, and when night fell again and the blanket of darkness lay over the cemetery, they met once more.

The ghoul was not where it had been the previous night, but it was not long until they found it wreaking havoc.

"You two again!" The ghoul raged, leaping to its feet and tossing aside the human skull it had been playing with. "Let me teach you a lesson."

"No, let us teach you a lesson." Dean smiled his eyes sparkling.

"Go on then, do your worse," the ghoul threatened with a sneer. It held out its large hands, claws dirty from where it had been digging.

Jasmine and Dean glanced at each other, nodded, then turned back to the ghoul, who was losing its patience with the children.

Jasmin reached slowly up and grabbed the sides of her head and, with a tug, she pulled it off. The ghoul screamed and fell over backwards, its dark eyes wide.

"That will teach you," Dean spat at the creature as, in one swift movement, he grabbed his hair and tore the entire skin off his head, revealing a gleaming white skull with bulging eyes.

The Ghoul shrieked and backed away until it stumbled into an old gravestone.

"We did warn you," Jasmine said, holding her head out to the cowering ghoul. "Now, be gone and don't ever return." And, squeezing her head, one eyeball shot out and landed on the ground by the ghoul.

That was all that it took for the creature, who leapt up and raced away screaming, its long arms flailing. Dean and Jasmin laughed happily as the horrid ghoul disappeared.

"That will teach that rotten thing," Dean chuckled, slipping his skin back on over his head like a child would with a hood.

Jasmine fitted her head back on.

"Sure will. Did you see the look on its face?" Jasmin said, bending over and picking up her eyeball. She blew some dirt from it before pushing it back into the socket, where it went with a squelching noise.

They laughed again as an owl swooped overhead.

"Well, hopefully the children will not be afraid anymore," Jasmine remarked.

"Sure, now how about a game of hide and seek?"

"Oh, ok then. But no hiding in any graves — including your own."

"Oh, alright," Dean said, and together they floated away towards the centre of the cemetery.

THE END

MOLLY

It was not right, not right at all.

Eliza lay in her bed listening to the commotion downstairs. Riley was protesting, his voice edged with anger as he shouted about his innocence. Mum and Dad were not having none of it.

Mum was very angry; her voice thundering through the floor of her bedroom. And she had a right to be angry too. It had been her car Riley had scratched up using one of the kitchen knives. Knives the children were forbidden from ever touching.

That was the last straw.

Riley was in serious trouble now.

Laying on her back, the seven-year-old wondered what punishment her parents would dish out to her brother. Would they really send him away to boarding school as they had threatened?

He was out of control and his behaviour scared her very much. First stealing, then smashing up the computer and electronics, and then throwing paint all over their parents' bedroom. And now he had gone and damaged mum's car. That was the final straw, as their parents had said.

"And he says that it was your fault Molly," Eliza spoke softly, turning her head to the figure who lay beside her.

Molly lay on her back, her soft hair spread out under her plastic head, her glassy eyes staring up at the ceiling, which was bleached in the soft blue glow of the night light.

Eliza had been given Molly after her father had bought a storage container from an auction. The family had gone down while he had broken the lock and entered the container. Apart from some old and broken furniture there had been nothing of value, but, at the very back, Riley had discovered the life-sized doll wrapped in plastic sheeting and heavily taped up with silver duct tape.

"You really want that ugly thing?" Riley had asked, with a disgusted look upon his face. But Eliza had, and her parents allowed her to keep the doll who she called Molly — for that was the name written on the label of the dress she wore. And soon she and Molly were best of friends, playing together, having tea parties, picnics with her teddy bears and drawing pictures. Whenever her friends came over, Molly was much envied.

But after a week or two, Riley's behaviour started to change. First, he claimed that something kept coming into his bedroom at night and, one night, after waking to see a shadow of someone hurrying out, accused her of being the culprit.

It had certainly not been her, she protested. Her parents let the matter drop, but a few days later dad's car keys went missing and were found in Riley's school bag. And then other stuff such as lunchboxes and books disappeared, and then mum had some money stolen out of her purse. All the items were found either on Riley or in his bedroom. Riley pleaded innocent to the thefts but was grounded.

He threatened to set up a camera, but one night shortly afterwards he ended up using a hammer from the toolbox to smash up the home PC, mum's laptop, mum and dad's phones and tablets. When their parents went to confront the boy, Riley was asleep in bed but the hammer was on his beside cabinet. A shouting match which had terrified Eliza erupted between them all as her brother pleaded his innocence. She knew her parents were growing ever more concerned by Riley's erratic behaviour; he was only ten after all.

"And then he went and blamed you, Molly." Eliza spoke softly. She turned her head and stared at her doll beside her. "How could he blame you Molly?"

She turned on her back and gazed at the ceiling while the commotion downstairs got a lot more aggressive. She did not like it when her family argued or fought — not at all.

Maybe Riley was jealous. That was what she had suggested to her mum. After all, there had been nothing for him in that storage container, only a doll for her. And he had taken a keen dislike to Molly ever since, calling her horrid names such as ugly, freaky and horrible.

But why such a reaction?

At first her parents claimed that it was his age, that he was rebellious. But after the computer business, Riley was walking a thin line. And then, the weekend just gone, while Eliza had been out with her parents shopping and Riley had been over a friend's house, someone had let themselves into their house and empty an entire can of red paint from their shed all over mum and dad's bedroom. It had splattered all over their bed, halfway up the walls, over their furniture and over the carpet. They had even splattered paint onto Molly too!

Molly had been found on the floor of her parents' bedroom with her beautiful hair speckled with paint as well as the bottom of her shoes which had left footprints all over the floor

Riley had a key to the house and although his friend had claimed that they had both been in the park, dad had found one of his shirts in the laundry basket splattered with red paint.

"I swear! It was not me!" he shouted, and he was almost in tears. He escaped punishment but was warned that was his last chance.

And now that had gone.

Eliza rolled around in her bed, gazing across at her wall. From downstairs something banged – most likely the door which her brother sometimes kicked in his rage – and now dad's voice was thundering.

Mum had just left them alone for a few minutes earlier that day. Eliza was fine; she was laying on the floor in the living room watching the television while Molly was sitting on the sofa behind her. Riley, who had been in a surprisingly good spirits the last few days, was upstairs doing his homework. Dad had been out at work. But when mum returned less than fifteen minutes later, she saw the damage to her car which sat in their driveway with two flat tires and a kitchen knife sticking out from one of the ruined wheels. The same knife which had been used to scratch BAD BOY into the side of the car.

By now, from downstairs, it sounded as if Riley's rage had broken down into tears. Eliza heard him crying, but his emotion was doing nothing to smother the flames of anger which still raged in their parents. She heard her mum say sternly that a phone call would be made.

Eliza might hate her brother but she would miss him. He was, after all, her older brother.

"At least I got you, Molly," she said, laying still. "You will never leave me."

The bedcovers shifted as the doll slowly rolled over against her, one arm tenderly snaking over her waist.

THE END

ARE YOU SCARED YET?

The children sat in a circle in the middle of the bedroom floor; the curtains were open and a mild breeze drifted in from the night. The only light came from the torch which was passed from one to the other as they each told their stories.

Charlotte was currently entertaining the group, speaking in a hushed voice, her eyes wide and dazzling as she shone the beam of light up on her face, masking her features with a grotesque mix of illumination and shadows.

"...and, dangling from the cars doorhandle was a HOOK."

Two of the girls, Jill and Tracey, shrieked at the sudden shocking ending. Todd, on the other hand, groaned and shook his head in disappointment.

"I heard that one when I was six." He told the girl rather harshly.

"No, you did not." His sister, Jill, snapped back.

"Yes, I did!" Todd snapped back, crossing his arms over his chest. "You girls tell such stupid stories. They are not even scary at all."

And it was true. At least when he had his friends sleep over, they all told each other excitingly scary stories. Not stupid ones that were either old or did not make any sense at all.

Charlotte looked rather disappointed.

"Ok. The Hook Man is a classic story from the 1950's, so three out of ten stars for you." Todd said to her. "But not scary."

Charlotte's face fell in annoyance.

"Well, maybe we should tell a true story?"

All eyes turned to the girl who had, until then, remained quiet. She had done so since turning up earlier that day, hardly speaking unless she had been spoken too. A girl who looked so misplaced at being invited to his sister's sleepover. She sat quietly in her sleeveless Mini Mouse nightie and had hardly reacted at all during the stories. Sally Watts, the odd girl, who Todd guessed had only been invited because their mum felt sorry for her.

"Ok then, let's see if you can keep me awake from this boredom."

Sally reached out her long, thin arm and took the torch from Charlotte. She was such a thin, pale girl.

Instead of shining the light up into her face, she turned and shone it gently over Todd's bedroom, highlighting his stacks of DVDs, comics and computer games that were piled in untidy stacks by the window and by his furniture across from his bed.

"There are creatures out there, small monsters with large heads, blazing eyes and wide mouths with sharp teeth." She spoke softly in her normal voice, not trying to build any atmosphere at all. But Todd was alert…so far.

"They have furry little bodies with claws on their hands and feet so they are able to climb up walls and across ceilings," Sally told them, her eyes darting between the others as they stared silently back at her. "They want children. No, they need children."

Todd licked his lips, he saw that the girls were all sitting quietly, Tracey looked scared.

"They will find a child who they think will be suitable and will then make their move. They will make their move and then, they befriend them."

Todd flinched as if he had been jolted, his heart dropped and he frowned in anger. He grunted loudly in disappointment; he had really thought that Sally was onto a good one.

"Todd!" Jill hissed angrily and punched him in the arm. A warning.

"Befriend! How utter—"

"Don't let that put you of." Sally turned to stare at him and he winced against the sudden glare of the torch. "For these are not creatures you would want as a friend. For they will be with you forever, never leaving your side, remaining with you until your dying breath."

Gasps from some of the girls, they all looked really scared now and Tracy Roberts looked as if she was shaking.

Todd rolled his eyes.

"Are you scared yet?" Sally asked.

"No."

Suddenly there was a clatter as a pile of comics and games toppled to the floor, one of the girls – Todd was unsure who – screamed as they all jumped up and turned towards the direction of the crash. Comics and DVDs lay scattered everywhere. Todd liked his DVDs, and although he was only 11, he had lots of them — mostly horror films that were rated 15 or 18. One of the DVDs had popped out of its case and now lay on the floor, the torchlight reflecting on its smooth silver side.

"You should be scared," Sally spoke almost breathlessly. "Because I saw one outside earlier when I arrived."

"Outside? Our house?" Jill asked sounding scared, and Todd noticed how she had pulled her pyjama top up to her face as if ready to hide her eyes. All the girls looked freaked out. Todd found it very amusing.

Sally nodded her head, her face blank and expressionless.

"Just maybe, it wants one of us to be its friend and it has been watching us all day long."

One of the other girls whimpered.

"Utter—"

A rustling, and Sally swung the light across the room and past Todd to where his bed stood against the far wall, the covers rumpled, a sheet hanging over the side.

"Are you scared yet?"

"Don't be daft."

"Then look, it is probably hiding under your bed."

At first Todd didn't move, but remained on his knees, staring at his bed. Then he reached out and snatched the torch from Sally's hands and started to crawl across the floor towards the bed. In his chest his heart began to pick up speed.

"Todd, no." Jill wailed and grabbed the waistband of his shorts. Todd pulled free and crawled across to his bed and leaned down low. Behind him the girls all cowered, quivering in fright apart from Sally, who sat a few inches away from the others, staring expressionlessly.

He turned back, reached out and grasped the hanging sheet, his hand shaking as he did. The torch suddenly felt very slippery in his other hand — he could feel cold sweat breaking out. His heart was thundering and his breath turned to ice.

"This is stupid," he said, more to himself than the girls.

He yanked the sheet up and the beam of the torch shone under his bed, at nothing at all.

With a smile, Todd allowed the sheet to fall back down then turned to the girls.

"See nothi—"

The bedroom door suddenly flung open and the children leapt to their feet in screams which echoed out into the night.

Todd and Jill's mother stood in the doorway, not at all looking amused.

"I hope you are not giving them nightmares," Mrs Eccles directed this comment towards her son. "Right, you girls should be in bed, so hurry along."

Wearily the girls all retreated out and Todd smirked as they went.

"I sure won't be having any nightmares," he said as they passed him, but by the looks on their faces, they sure would be.

"I do wish you wouldn't tell them scary stories, Todd," his mother moaned as she hurried across to his window, which she partly closed then pulled the curtains closed together. "And I do wish you would tidy up, such a mess."

"I will mum." Todd groaned, switching on his bedside light and sitting down on his bed. His mum hurried over and kissed him goodnight and left, closing his bedroom door.

Todd grunted and shuffled under his covers and switched off his bedside light, plunging his bedroom into darkness broken only by the glow from under his door. He could hear the faint sounds of his mum and the girls talking, one of them sounded upset and it made him laugh into his pillow.

Then he heard a shuffling noise, like tapping of feet racing across his floor. Todd was instantly alert, and then came a thump of something banging into his wardrobe.

Todd sat up and reached for his light. But there was no need.

From the dark corner of his bedroom, two glowing eyes stared back at him.

THE END

THE THING UPSTAIRS

Ok, let me start by telling you that our house was not haunted.

That during the first ten months after we had moved in, everything was well. Our new house was old but we soon got used to the creaking floorboards and the rattling of the pipes. Even Bradly, my annoying little brother, seemed to settle in rather well.

Everything was just fine until I found that cupboard.

That was when things went very, very bad.

Poor dad had his hands full raising us kids. Sophie was no help; she was thirteen years old and always on her phone chatting to her friends about boys at school or the latest K-pop bands. And Bradley could be a real pain in the butt but was, after all, only six. So it fell to me, the middle child, to help dad out with the decorating.

Dad wanted colours, bright colours that he associated with his Caribbean heritage. Dad was not born in the UK but he was raised here from an early age after his parents had emigrated. Dad was proud of his culture and ethnic background and raised us pretty much the same. Both dad and I had our long hair braided and I enjoyed the cuisines that he had inherited from his mum. He often cooked chicken or fish enriched with herbs and spices such as bell peppers, cassava, tomatoes, cilantro, coconut and sweet potatoes. I will openly admit that I love my food and would eat anything from brown stew chicken to a shepherd's pie. Bradley, on the other hand, enjoyed a Wimpy or

McDonald's while Sophie was trying – once again – to be a vegan.

So, there I was, helping dad stripping the faded old wallpaper from the upstairs landing outside of Bradley's bedroom, ready to slap on the bright oranges and reds that would brighten it up. And then I discovered it, just a corner at first. Frowning, I peeled away more paper and only then saw that my discovery was a door. The cupboard was at least four meters square and was set flat into the wall as if someone had re-plastered that part of the wall to hide the cupboard. There was no handle and a number of screws were dotted around the sides holding it firmly closed.

"What an odd place for a cupboard." Dad remarked after I had called him over.

"Do you think there is anything inside?" I asked curiously, my hands on my hips, the front of my T-shirt speckled with flakes of old, dusty wallpaper.

"Let's find out," Dad suggested patting me on the back.

He got a screwdriver from his toolbox and started work. The screws must have been in for a long time. They were very tight and dad had to work hard to get them free. His labours bought both Sophie and Bradly hurrying over to look.

Finally the last screw dropped to the ground.

"How do we open it?" Bradley asked, clutching his small rag teddy bear, Mr Chipps, firmly to his side.

"A screw should do the trick." Dad piped up. The door had a small hole where a handle once must have been, but why would anyone want to cover up a cupboard?

Dad made a handle with a screw and then pulled the door. It was stiff and he had to use a lot of force. The hinges squealed and dust coughed out, and as we gathered around poor Bradley had to stand on his tip toes for a better look.

But there was nothing in there at all. In fact the cupboard was so shallow you couldn't store anything in there, and the

35

sides and back were nothing but flaky plaster. Our disappointment must have shown.

"What's that?" Bradley noticed some marks on the inside of the door.

Three deep lines that looked like…

"Are those claw marks?" Sophie asked, astonished, and taking notice of something other than her phone for once in her life.

"No, just marks." Dad told her with a laugh, though they sure did look like claw marks.

Excitement over, we all scurried back to what we had been doing. The cupboard was so small and narrow that, at first, I thought there was no use for it. But by later that day, Bradley was in one of his moods and was annoying me so much that I snatched Mr Chipps from him and managed to stuff it inside that cupboard and slammed the door shut. Being short, Bradley was unable to reach the door, so he was not at all happy with me and became very angry.

"What is going on, Michelle?" Dad asked hurrying up the stairs as Bradley had a meltdown.

"I am trying to sort out my stuff and he keeps on annoying me."

"Is that right, Brad? Are you provoking your sister?" Dad crouched down to where Bradley was crying and shouting on the floor, his feet hammering on the wall that dad and I had stripped earlier that day, the sound thumping in my head.

Brad stopped, sniffed and nodded his head. Dad told me to get Mr Chipps so, with a defeated huff; I went over and opened the cupboard door.

Mr Chipps lay where I had put him, but he had been ripped apart.

*

Things got weirder from that night on.

I was in bed under my covers, secretly reading with the aid of the torch from my mobile, when there was a loud knock on my door which scared the life out of me. I called out but there was no answer so, believing it was just dad who had seen my light shining out from underneath the door when I should have been asleep, I put my book away and turned off my torch.

The knock came again, this time so much harder that my door shook in the frame, and I sat up, alert.

"Brad?" I called slipping out of bed. "Bradley?"

I heard the sound of heavy feet running away across the landing.

I bolted towards my door, pulling it open and smacking on my light at the same time. But the landing was deserted and the only sound I could hear was of dad laughing at some show on the television from downstairs.

I hurriedly passed both Sophie's and dad's bedrooms and ran into Bradley's room. His door was always open as he was afraid of being alone, but he lay fast asleep in his bed, and he was not faking either. I could tell by the sound of his breathing. I backed out and looked around but nobody was there. The small cupboard door that had been closed earlier was now open ajar.

*

The following day nobody believed me when I mentioned what had occurred last night. But things got a lot stranger. Sophie's homework, which she had left on her desk, got torn up. Pages shredded, scrunched and ripped were scattered over her desk and bedroom floor. Dad was not happy at all and both Brad and I got accused, but we were innocent. Then Brad's toys ended up scattered all over the landing and he swore that he had not done it and, somehow, I believed him.

For the first time I started to get chills being upstairs, the entire atmosphere had changed. It no longer felt warm and safe but cold, and I always felt as if I was being watched. That small cupboard was always ajar too, no matter how many times I would slam it shut.

That night Bradley could not sleep. He claimed that he could hear knocking from his wall right where the cupboard was located. Dad tried soothing him, but every time Brad fell asleep and dad returned back to his room, Bradly was woken up once again. In the end, he slept in dad's bedroom.

And after I had finally fallen back to sleep after that commotion, I was awoken up in the early hours of the morning feeling bitterly cold. My windows were wide open and my bedcovers had been pulled off, and, to my horror, now lay heaped in the corner of my room. I glanced at my bedroom door to find that it was open.

I never slept with my bedroom door open.

*

"Well, it wasn't me!" Sophie defended herself at breakfast after I had told her of what had happened.

"Then who?" I challenged her angrily. Dad held his hands out and we stopped our bickering.

"Whatever is going on between you both, it has to stop," Dad ordered sternly. Sophie and I glanced at each other in defeat.

I blamed it all on the cupboard. Ever since I'd found it, all these strange things were happening. Our stuff kept on disappearing and reappearing in different places, footsteps on the landing, and things getting torn apart. I told my family that all this started when we had found that cupboard and had opened the door, but dad did not believe me. Only one person believed me...Brad.

That night Bradley fell asleep in my room, so dad had carried him back to his own room and tucked him into bed. I was just finishing stitching up Mr Chipps when I needed to go to the toilet. It was pretty late but, being a Saturday, we never had a set bedtime. Everyone was asleep, the house was quiet.

I stepped out of my bedroom, leaving my door open slightly so that the light would flood out into the landing. Thankfully my room was next to the bathroom. I hurriedly did my business, flushed and washed my hands, switched off the light as I stepped straight out of the bathroom...and into darkness.

My bedroom door was closed and the light was off. The landing was so dark and cold that even my bare feet felt frozen on the floorboards. Before I could think, the light behind me flickered on and off before going out once again, plunging me back into a nightmarish darkness where I could not see my own hand in front of my face.

From further along the landing a floorboard squeaked. I was frozen, gripped in a fear that was as cold as I felt. And, from close by, I could hear breathing. A shallow, nasal type of breathing that sounded frightful and evil.

My heart started to hammer in my chest and my throat went dry and the back of my neck began to tingle. I was so scared that I can't put into words how I felt.

"Dad," I called out, my voice tight and small in my throat. The breathing became louder with excitement, as if this thing liked my fear, my panic.

From behind something brushed my long, braided hair — cold long fingers twirled around.

"DAD." Louder, but still a croak.

The hand in my hair tightened and pulled and I screamed as my scalp burned as my head was forced back.

My knees buckled and I dropped to the floor. I was being pulled around by my hair and I started to scream in fear and pain.

Dad's bedroom light flicked on and I heard Bradley call out, but I could not hear his words through my screaming as I was wrenched around and was half dragged, half crawled along the landing towards their bedrooms.

Dad's door opened and I was finally released, and crying I rushed into his arms. Bradley and Sophie stood looking on afraid.

But the safety I felt was short lived, for suddenly Bradley's door was slammed shut, sealing my brother inside, and he started to scream and hammer on the door with his fists. Sophie wrapped her arms around me and we watched in terror as dad hurried over to Bradley's aid. At first, he could not get it open, and from inside Brad was screaming and crying and there were sounds of his furniture being thrown about.

Finally dad threw himself at the door and managed to force it open and Bradley raced out into his arms. Toys were thrown out after him as an evil laugh filled the air and Sophie and I screamed. The light flickered and went out, plunging us into darkness once again.

With Brad in his arms Dad ushered us into his room, where he slammed the door shut. We leapt onto his bed and the four of us huddled together as the thing crashed about outside on the landing, raking the doors and walls with its claws and banging on the walls. The vibrations shook the bed where we huddled, jolting us up and down. Even dad was screaming and I had never heard him sound scared before, which made me feel even more frightened. We all screamed, we cried and we shook. Finally the thing settled down and it all went quiet.

Dad moved quickly, climbing down from the bed. We did not want him to go, but he told us to stay where we were as he was going to put an end to all of this.

41

We watched wide eyed as he got his screwdriver from his overturned toolbox and some screws and headed out into the landing, switching on the light and keeping the door open. We heard him slam the cupboard door shut and then he got to work.

On legs that felt stiff and shaky, I pulled away from my siblings and climbed down from the bed. Sophie reached for me, but I hurried to the doorway and watched as dad screwed shut the cupboard door.

Done, dad and I re-joined the others and we all embraced in the middle of the room, relieved that the nightmare was over.

Then Sophie went rigid and I felt her catch her breath. We all turned to the wall where she stared in wide-eyed fright. Towering over us was the silhouette of a hunched creature with long slender arms and long cold clawed fingers.

Dad had not locked the thing back into the cupboard, but had locked it out with us.

THE END

HIGH TIDE

The sea was angry.

Jacob Miller watched as the waves crashed to the stony shore with a roar. Pellets of foamy spittle spraying out as the water gushed ashore, rolling the shells and cobbles, making them rattle like bones. And the way the tide withdrew with an angry sigh, only to unleash its fury a second later with another wave made the boy even more wary about the water then he already felt.

In the distance, boats sat hazed by a mist that slowly crept in, carried by the wind that blew around them.

"Did I tell you about the children who drowned?" Eddie asked Jake who turned away from the angry sea to face the tallest boy of the group. They were all ten years old, but Eddie was the oldest of them all.

"Don't tell him that one," Amy complained, pulling a face.

"Why not?" Max asked, bouncing his red ball at his side and not really paying much attention to them. All he wore was a white vest which fluttered noisily around his frame, and shorts. Jake could not understand how he did not feel the cold.

The four of them stood together on the almost empty stretch of beach. The wind whipping around them, tugging at their clothing and pulling at their hair, and Jake tried his best not to look too cold in front of them in the T-shirt and fleece that he wore. They did not seem too fazed by the cold chill the wind carried but, yet again, they were all local, born and bred to the countryside and used to the elements of the passing seasons. Jake, however, was born and raised in a town and had only moved down to the area before the summer. He was still getting used to country life and, maybe, he would never get used to it! Although he and his family had been welcomed warmly by the community, he did not believe he would settle in well in his new, rural surroundings and environment.

During the summer, the stony shore would have been littered with sunbathers and families at play who would travel down to spend the day at South Haven Bay's beach. But now, in late September, the beach was empty except for the occasional dog walker or local youths such as themselves. South Haven Bay was only a small coastal village which offered nothing to attract tourism, which, for the locals, was fine. Attention was not wanted and not needed; the village thrived on serving the local villagers or visitors from the villages further inland.

"Best he knows all the stories," Eddie smirked, his blue eyes shimmering and long brown hair blowing beneath his red beany hat. He wore a black T-shirt with the logo of some heavy metal band and trousers that were ripped at the knees. A jacket was tied around his narrow waist.

Jake sighed and thought why not. Eddie and others at school had taken great delight in telling him about people falling from the clifftops or swimmers disappearing out at sea.

"About ten years ago, three children and a teenager went out on their dingy," Eddie told Jake, fixing him intently with his eyes, the freckles that speckled his face seeming to darken. "But a storm suddenly came in…."

"Just like this one!" Max added, holding his ball firmly to his side. Amy turned to him and pulled a face; she wore shorts and a black sleeveless T-shirt with boots which any goth would have admired.

Jake glanced again at the sea with its high rolling waves that crashed against the shore. Clouds hung low in the sky, heavy and burdened by the brewing storm.

"And the children were swept out at sea," Eddie continued.

Jake turned back and wiped his running nose with his sleeve. He could feel speckles of moisture spraying him and was unsure if it was the sea or rain.

"All the children perished and their bodies were never found."

"They are still out there." Max commented, quietly bouncing his ball on the stony beach as they all turned to watch the high, crashing waves of the uncaring sea.

"Sure are," Eddie agreed with a smile. "Because during stormy, misty weathers – like now – it's said that you can hear the distant shouts and screams of the dead children."

And then Eddie started to call out in a ghostly voice and Amy playfully punched him on the shoulder. Jake shivered, more from the cold than anything else, he had heard many such stories and did not really care or believe them.

Max kicked the ball up and they started to pass it to and from each other, spreading out on the lonely beach. Eddie kicked hard and Jake jumped, but the ball sailed over his reaching hands. Jake turned in time to see it hit the sea with a plop.

"Now you've done it!" Eddie shouted, annoyed. "Quickly, go get it!"

"No. Don't," Amy warned, marching over.

"Yes, he lost it — he can get it."

Turning back to the sea, Jake watched as the waves pushed the ball as if in game. It was not far; he could get it! No worries. He couldn't show his fear to the others.

"Its dangerous out there," Amy warned.

But Jake was already at work, crouching down and removing his socks and shoes and pulling up his trouser legs as high as they would go. In his chest his heart was hammering.

He started to head out, the stones feeling cold under his feet until he reached the ones that were wet. A wave crashed to shore and water gushed inwards and over his feet and Jake cried out and hopped about from foot to foot. The sea felt as cold as ice.

Sucking in a deep breath he waddled further out and held his breath as another wave sloshed over his legs. He could feel bits of stone and grain hitting his feet, the current was strong and he felt the force of it pulling. But feet away was Max's ball, which seemed so much further than he had first thought.

He glanced behind him, wondering if the others were watching, but they were joking around with each other — Amy had her phone out and was filming Eddie and Max's antics.

He started to wade further out, and another wave hit him, so forcefully that he almost toppled backwards. Water splashed around his knees, struck his chest, and stung his face. He licked his lips and tasted the strong tang of salt. One trouser leg fell down but he did not care, he was wet anyway.

The mist was creeping in. Now he could not even see the boats that sat out at sea. Directly in front, the sea was dragging the ball further out, it was just beyond his arms reach, maybe another step...

The wave crashed into him just as he lifted his foot, so forceful that Jake could not keep his balance. He was thrown down backwards, arms twirling and mouth open in a scream which was snatched away as he hit the water. The dark coldness closed around, gushing loudly into his ears and burning his sinuses as he choked. He kicked and flayed and burst out with a shuddering gasp, only for another wave to crash over him and dunk him under again into its merciless cold murky depths. He could taste the sea as it gushed into his mouth and burned his

46

throat, and his cold body went numb as panic struck him. He kicked his feet and felt no ground; he had been pulled too far out. He kicked and battled frantically against the undercurrent and burst out, gasping for air.

Where was Eddie and the others? Hopefully they had… But even in his panic he saw that the mist had drawn in around him, cloaking him in its fine shroud. He wanted to scream, he wanted to shout and to cry, but he couldn't. Another wave crashed over him but, somehow, he remained above the surface. But his body was wrecked by the coldness, and he shuddered and hitched as he sucked in breath and his arms and legs felt like lead, not helped by his sodden clothing which was weighing him down.

Voices…

Yes, he could hear voices of children. He bobbed up to avoid a wave and stayed with his head above the water, the sea roared in his ears, but he was sure he heard voices, inaudible, but — and there, far out to his right, he saw a dark shadow hidden behind the mist. He blinked his eyes and saw the blurred shape of a boat and four hunched figures huddled together staring back at him.

"Hel—" In desperation he held out one heavy arm and a wave crashed over him, plunging him under its cold depth, and Jake felt himself swirling and turning in all directions, his arms and legs thrashing weakly out under the heavy current and his drenched clothing. He glanced up at the shimmering light above and saw the hand reaching down towards his. He felt those fingers enclosing his wrist and actually felt how much colder that hand was compared to the sea. He was pulled, and his legs kicked feebly until he burst up, choking and spluttering as he leant against the side of the dingy. He choked and rolled his head back and stared up at the figure who had saved him.

The hand that still held him tightly belonged to a boy his own age, or maybe slightly older, it was impossible to tell. The

47

boy stared down with his one white eye; the other was just a large empty, gaping hole. His blue tinged skin was mottled and transparent in places; in others it had peeled away to expose bone. His dark hair was plastered to his head and his lips were peeled back, exposing crooked teeth.

The smell of rot filled his lungs as Jake struggled for breath, and a sudden feeling of panic and terror flared through him and he tried to pull free, forgetting about his own peril. But the boy in the dingy held on and Jake felt himself being pulled up against the faded yellow boat that stayed full and afloat despite the worn patches and gaping holes on its sides.

The other children leaned over and reached down with their skeletal arms and clawed fingers. Jakes own hand clutched his saviour's arm so tightly that he felt the wet flesh pulling away from the bone.

He was hauled up and over into the wide dingy, where he lay gasping, his wide eyes glaring at the children as they crowded around him. The boy who had rescued him only wore red trunks, patches of his skin was so thin and worn that they hung from his bones like old rags, and Jake saw that most of the boy's right ribcage was exposed and mottled with seaweed.

Beside him a tall girl watched blankly, her lips, chin and nose rotted down to the bone while the girl beside her was nothing more than a skeleton with bulging white eyes. The second boy stared back in silence, his broken jaw hanging against his chest.

Jake stared at each of them before he passed out.

*

Jake opened his eyes and found himself flat on his back on the beach, the sea sloshing around his outstretched feet. He was wet and cold and his body was shaking with deep tremors that he could not control despite the jacket that had been thrown over and tucked in around him. Eddie, Max and Amy looked down at him, their faces etched with concern and fright. Even Eddie looked scared. Overhead the sky was dark and rain fell in heavy drops.

"Are you ok?" Amy asked, sounding frightful, rubbing his chest. "What happened?"

Then they were all speaking at once. Jakes head spun. He made out that they had called 999.

"You sure must be a good swimmer," Eddie said, rather impressed.

"They saved me, the children. They were dead," Jake told them, though his voice felt horse and weak.

With Amy and Max's help he sat up and stared out at the mist where he could hear the sound of the crashing waves.

"Who?" Max asked.

"The children Eddie spoke about…they…"

"Just a ghost story, Jake." Eddie told him with a shrug. "They died years ago; they don't—"

"Look!" Amy pointed and they all saw the dark silhouette hidden beneath the retreating mist. The shadow where the children's giggling could be heard. And then they all watched as Max's ball was thrown out towards them, bouncing once on the stone beach and coming to a rest by Jake's feet.

THE END

THE SCARECROWS

During the daytime the sun had blazed down onto the fields and ignited the wheat in gold. But now, under the moonlight's glare, the wheat looked dull, as if rotten or diseased. The whole landscape seemed sinister at night, then it did during the day.

Ash stood on the bottom rung of the barred gate, staring across at the vast field of crops. A damp breeze blew, combing through the soft, fluffy heads of the wheat, the sounds they made always seemed eerie to the young boy. He did not want to admit that he was feeling a bit nervous and glad that nobody was around to see him looking so apprehensive.

He licked his lips and, despite the warmth of summers night, shuddered in the T-shirt which he had hastily slipped on. The smell of the breeze was sickly sweet with the wheat and the damp soil – a country smell – his mum often told him, before saying how good and healthy it was for him, but Ash did not like it.

It was late, the time had gone half ten when he had sneaked out, and it was certainly no place for a nine-year-old boy to be out on his own. From all around nothing stirred, the flat plains of farmlands and fields seemed as derelict of life as those scenic paintings in the gallery's his mum used to take him to before they had moved away from London.

In his chest his heart was beating as fast as a train, his eyes scanned the field before him and paused on one of the isolated figures that stood above the fluffy crop closest to him.

Scarecrows.

From the distance, they were nothing more than dark shapes scattered about the field, rooted in their places on their posts, with their outstretched arms creaking as they swayed gently in the sweet breeze.

The one closest to the gate was the smallest, with a head made from a potato sack with button eyes that had been stitched on wide and crooked, and a mouth that split across its face. Its clothing was so old that it hung in torn tatters, and straw and hay poked through.

Going by the local children, the scarecrows like to jump down from their posts and hunt people for their skins. This idea was supported by the Green brothers – Toby and Donovan – the two boys from the farm and who were the only friends he had made since moving down to Devon.

Ash had shaken his head, unsure what to make of that, and decided to ignore it altogether. He came from a serious family; his father, whom he hardly ever saw these days, was a serious man from Pakistan currently living in Luton with a new family. His mum, who was originally from Swansea, loved the classical arts and preferred a scenic and peaceful way of life. Neither his parents tolerated any jokes or made-up stories told by children.

Taking a deep breath, Ash swung his leg over the top of the gate and dropped down to the ground. He turned to face the crops and, for the first time, he felt a strong fear grip him. The wheat looked much darker and taller now that he was standing three feet away —over a meter high and he would only just be able to see over their swaying heads.

He did not really want to cut across the crops to the field beyond, but had no choice — it would be a lot quicker. If his mum ever discovered that he had sneaked out she really would be mad with him — she would kill him!

The boy hoped that she was still sitting out in the garden admiring the stars and drinking wine with her boyfriend. Perhaps she would never find out about his little expedition.

Shaking his long black fringe from his eyes, Ash started forward and parted the wheat with his arms as he stepped inside. The stick-like stems felt stiff and bristly, the fluffy heads rustling together as he stepped through, his trainers trampling on some of their bases and breaking them. There was a wide path further along, but he did not want to delay his quest for any longer than necessary as, in his chest, he could feel his fear building.

The wheat closed tightly around him as he trekked slowly through the crops, heavy heads swinging and pelting his face. He spat as one wiped across his mouth leaving behind a bitter seed of grain. The noise he made seemed extra loud in the stillness of the night.

His foot suddenly caught on a fallen stem, almost tripping him, and he swore under his breath. Maybe he should just leave his jacket and find it tomorrow, but he knew that if his mum ever found it was missing and knew that his keys were in the pocket then…

From somewhere nearby came a heavy crunch, which reminded him of the time he had watched the Green brothers throwing huge blocks of straw down from the top of the loft in their barn. That was what it sounded like.

Ash paused and his breath caught in his throat, and his heart skipped a beat; he turned, scanning all around him, but saw nothing. He even rose up on his tiptoes, and all around the crops swayed in the breeze. Gritting his teeth he started forward once again only, this time, going a bit quicker.

Finally, after what seemed like a lifetime, he emerged out of the crops and hurried across to the stone wall. Beyond, the bow of the hill was bathed in the glow of moonlight, and he saw the trees and the huge stone boulder that looked much further away than it was.

He climbed over the wall, feeling the grit beneath his hands and, as fast as he could, he raced across the hill which rose up towards the night sky. He was breathless by the time he reached the huge stone, but not wishing to dwell to catch his breath, he hurried around the boulder until he came across his denim jacket that had fallen to the grassy ground. He snatched it up and with relief found the front door key in the breast pocket.

It had been a hot day, so Ash had taken off his jacket when he had met up with Toby and Donovan earlier and they had wandered into the wheat to play hide and seek. Ash had forgotten all about his jacket when they had headed back to the Green farm for an ice cream and a cold drink. He would not have worried but he had been given the front door key by his mum after all the protesting he had done and of promises he had made to her about being reliable.

With his jacket in one hand and key clutched tightly in the other, Ash sprinted back down to the field and climbed up onto the wall. He stood shakily on top and staring out across the field of wheat so that he could catch his frantic breaths, his long black hair was stuck to his neck and his mouth felt dry and coppery. Then he frowned when, ahead in the distance, he saw that one of the scarecrows posts was empty.

He was not worried, maybe it had blown down by the wind. Going by the Green brothers, the scarecrows were often found crumpled on the ground by their posts, they were not really looked after at all.

Ash leapt down and re-entered the crops. The wheat rustled loudly as it enclosed around him, showering seed over his shoulders, arms and legs as he frantically battled his way through, his feet snapping and crunching the stems.

He paused as he heard a different sound.

It was like someone or something making their way through the wheat.

Ash rose up on his tiptoes and turned towards the sound, and his heart jumped in his chest when he saw the wheat ahead swaying as something moved through it. And it was heading towards him.

From behind came another sound just like he heard from moments before, and he turned sharply and saw, further along in the distance that another scarecrow had fallen from its post.

A strong feeling of fear and dread gripped him, and he wanted to scream but his throat felt tightened. He started to hurry, battling through the wheat, panting loudly in fear and exhaustion. His foot caught something and he fell to his hands and knees, though thankfully the earth was soft and he was unhurt. But he heard the sounds of something hurrying after him, moving quicker now, it sounded closer.

Ash climbed to his feet, snatched up his jacket and started to battle his way through the wheat, his arms waving wildly to clear a path, his breaths coming out in dry whimpers.

Was he going the right way?

He was moving so frantically that he was unsure which direction he was heading in now and did not want to waste time to check. Wheat whipped across his cheek so hard that it stung, but Ash did not want to stop. From the sound of it his pursuer was catching up, moving hidden in the wheat, moving at a great speed.

Then his jacket snagged on something and almost slipped free from his hand. Ash turned and cried out in horror.

The small scarecrow stood on its stick-like legs, one arm raised, gloved hand clutching at his jacket, its mouth open revealing the hay and straw embedded in its head. And Ash did scream, his scream tearing out into the silent night and reaching only a lone badger and a herd of deer resting beneath a tree on the field.

Ash staggered backwards. His hand slipped free from his jacket, and his heels snagged on a root and fell onto his back, crunching wheat as he went. His wide brown eyes stared up in fright at the scarecrow as it took one huge, clumsy step towards him and then another, one hand holding his jacket, the other reaching down to where he lay.

Ash screamed, shoving himself back with his hands and heels, throwing up dirt as he went, sliding back before rolling over onto his hands and knees. He was sure he felt a hand grasp the back of his jeans, and he screamed again as he flung himself up and forwards, battling away through the wheat, trampling the stalks down as he frantically fought his way forward. His body was wracked by shudders of fright as he went, tears streaming down his face his heart pulsed furiously in his chest.

He glanced back over his shoulder and ran into the figure ahead so hard that straw burst from the front of its tatty shirt. But the impact did little to shift it from where it stood, and Ash staggered back from the much taller scarecrow with the old pumpkin head and into the smaller one that clutched at his shoulder with its free gloved hand. Ash screamed and fought but the scarecrow held him tightly and firmly, it did not even budge under his frantic struggling.

From all around other scarecrows approached from different directions, closing in on him in a tight circle on their stick legs.

"Let go! Let go!" Ash screamed over and over as he tugged frantically. His shirt tore, and, in frustration, he pulled his T-shirt up to his chin and wiggled himself free, dropping face first to the ground and rolling over onto his back. He stared up at the scarecrows as they circled around him, trapping him with

their creaking bodies. The small scarecrow stood by his feet, holding his jacket in one hand and T-shirt in the other and, through his fear, Ash saw the smile widen on its face as it held up the clothing.

Then the others leaned down and Ash sank to the ground, raising his arms up to shield himself as they reached for him.

*

Ash did not see anyone as he made his way home.

That was good, he did not want to explain why he was out in the middle of the night with nothing on but socks and his marooned coloured pants.

He was unsure what the time was, but his house was dark and his mum was not in the garden. She had locked up before going to bed and had probably seen his key missing from the hook, but that was fine, he would just tell her that he had left it in his pocket.

What he could not explain, however, if anyone was to notice, was how the small scarecrow in the wheat field was now perched on its post dressed smart in his own jeans, trainers, T-shirt and jacket, and had a wide smile stitched upon its face.

THE END

THE FORBIDDEN WOODS

The snowball sailed through the cold crisp air and struck Hector Dorothy on the chest.

"Yes!" Jamie Daniels shouted jumping up, his gloved fists punching the air. "England one, Scotland nil."

"Bah!" Hector spat brushing snow from his jacket. "Ye wish! Scotland 5 rounds, England 2."

Jamie mock laughed as Hector walked over, his booted feet kicking up snow, his cheeks and nose as red as his jacket. A tuft of fringe poking out from beneath his blue hat was stuck across his forehead in a wet strand.

The village of Jordeen was in the north-east of Scotland, sitting on the plains of the Highlands. To the northwest lay High Loch Wood, a remnant of the once endless Caledonian Forest, with its countless pine trees, oaks, ash, elms and elders.

The snow had fallen gracefully throughout the night, carpeting the landscape in all of its glorious white. The vast field where the friends played had been like a sheet of paper, smooth and glossy, and was broken now only by their games.

The cold was fresh and raw, and their breath vapoured in the air like smoke. In the distance the peaks and rolls of the mountains were nothing more than hazed shapes in the sky where the low grey clouds promised fresh snow for tonight, possibly even sooner.

"Fancy a game o' footie?" Hector suggested, standing in

front of his friend.

Jamie sniffed loudly and shook his head.

"You know I can't play football in these wellies."

A smile lit up Hector's face.

"What a pathetic excuse. We a' know that is coz us Scots are better at footie."

Jamie gave his friend a playful shove and before long, both boys were shoving and shouldering each other and the quiet air was alive with the sounds of their laughter and boisterous mocking.

Hector spoke with a strong Glaswegian accent where Jamie had a soft southern tone, though he could still pronounce certain words correctly, such as 'Loch' rather than saying 'Lock', which is a common mispronunciation for the English.

Hector lived in one of the bungalows that backed onto the field, hidden under the heaped snow, and Jamie loved visiting his friend at this time of the year when the rawness of the Scottish winters offered extensive snowfall. Across the field were the woods, the bare trees that lined the bleak woodlands stood holding up a roof of snow, their trunks glazed — it was such a pretty sight, one Jamie admired.

For the past four years, ever since his family moved from Glasgow and settled in Surrey, where he had been born, Jamie always visited his friend in the winter while Hector visited every summer. It was their tradition and one the two 11-year-olds kept solid. It was even better since the Dorothy's had moved to the Highlands.

Hector suggested he would go get a ball from home so they could take aim at some posts they would make from snow and see who could knock down the most.

Jamie thought that was a great idea and asked if he should start making up some posts further down the field.

"Aye, mind an' keep away from the woods!" It was a rule that they were not allowed in the woods, one Mr and Mrs

60

Dorothy reminded him every time he visited.

As Hector trudged wearily back up across the slight bow of the field towards the bungalows, Jamie turned and made his way down towards the woodlands, where the snow had not been disturbed. He loved the sounds his feet made crunching in the snow and he took giant steps.

High above a bird of prey soared and Jamie glanced up, turning so his back was to the woods, backing up and watching as it flew across the icy sky.

He wondered what kind of bird it was, Hector would know.

He watched as his breath swirled up, and, sucking in a deep lungful of breath, blew deeply out, watching as the vapour swirled and clouded up like smoke before disappearing. He was like a dragon, a fierce dragon blowing smo…

A snowball suddenly smashed into the back of his head so forcefully that he staggered forward, his hat almost falling off. Slushy snow sloshed over his cheek and slid between his scarf and collar; one slither even touched the nape of his neck causing him to shiver.

He spun around on his booted heels, expecting to see Hector standing there between two trees pointing and laughing, but there was nobody.

From eight feet away, the trees lay silent and still, not even nature stirred.

"Heck, you creep," he shouted, his voice loud in the stillness. "Where are you?"

Silence.

Nothing stirred.

A small chunk of snow fell from one of the branches.

"Heck?" Surely Hector hadn't doubled back when he wasn't looking?

Jamie turned back and ran his eyes over the field but, apart from his own tracks, he saw no sign that Hector had done such

such a thing.

A second snowball struck his back, followed by a third which exploded on the back of his head. That last one had been hard and had actually stung.

Jamie spun around to face the woodlands, his eyes scanning through the first row of trees and into the wilds beyond, but he only saw the empty woodlands.

"Heck?" He walked forward towards the woods, a puzzled expression on his face.

"Hector?"

He came to a stop between two trees. Inside the woodlands the ground was not as thick with snow, and he saw the humps of twisted tree roots coiling up from the uneven ground, small whisps of snowflakes drifted down from the towering canopy above.

Then, from within the denseness, he heard the giggling of children.

"Hector?"

Unsure, Jamie took a step, his boot crunching both snow and foliage. It might not be Hector, but most likely other children from the village who knew well enough that they were not allowed to play in the woods.

Maybe Angus or Freya from a few doors down from the Dorothy's?

They were pretty mischievous at times.

He called out their names.

More giggling came, but it sounded further away. His feet crunched as he slowly went further into the woodland, moving towards where the sound had come from and almost tripping over a snared root; daylight dwindled the further he went, the trees seemed to swarm, enclosing him, and the smell of wet leaves and decaying foliage was strong in the air. The woods smelt damp and nothing moved, not even a bird.

His breath came in damp pants as he hurried his pace up,

following the sounds of the childish giggling that seemed to come from all around, yet always sounding further and further away.

He hurried up a slight hill and rested against a tree, his eyes scanning the darkening woods. From his left came a heavy sloshing sound of snow dropping, just like when Mr Dorothy cleared the snow from his car.

Then, from the right a branch cracked and Jamie snapped his head around, but saw no one. From further ahead there was more giggling, but this time it did not sound so friendly.

A shiver cascaded down his spine and his heart skipped a beat, a heavy feeling of fear overcoming him. He suddenly felt very alone.

Then, from behind, a hand grasped his shoulder.

Jamie screamed and Hector shushed him, his gloved hand tightening on his padded shoulder. Relieved, Jamie turned his head to his friend, who was staring straight ahead with narrowed eyes.

"Don't move, Jamie," he spoke low but firmly, his face serious. "It's looking at us."

"Who?" Jamie asked, turning back and scanning the woodlands.

He saw the figure just as Hector spoke.

"The snowman."

Up ahead, far in the distance amid the dim light a solitary white figure stood upright beside a crooked tree. Jamie was too far away to see the detail but it was defiantly a snowman.

He smiled suddenly, feeling rather foolish.

"Good try, Heck but…"

Hector was not the best at making jokes, never had been since nursery school, and Jamie saw that his friend was serious.

His face was pale, his gaze firm, blue eyes shimmering with fear — it suddenly sent a chill of fear deep down Jamie's body.

"Make nae sudden movements Jamie. Just back away."

Jamie turned back to the snowman and, to his horror, saw that it had moved and now stood metres away, much closer to where they were. He saw the dirt and leaves that covered its body, its black stone eyes and rotted carrot nose. His heart leapt and his knees suddenly went weak, a cold feeling settled in the pit of his stomach.

"Hector, what's going on?" his voice tremored with panic. He went to turn to his friend, but Hector started to pull him back and Jamie followed on feet that felt just as rubbery as his wellies.

"It moved! it has…"

"Aye, just listen to me Jamie, an' do as I say."

A snowball flew out from their left and exploded into the tree trunk above their heads and both boys ducked, but Hector never released Jamie, never even stopped moving, stumbling slowly backwards. Jamie felt so cold that he struggled to move, and resisted the urge to turn and run.

The snowman had gone from in front of them, and Jamie scanned the woodlands and saw it standing to their right, now even closer. And, to his left, he saw a second figure, seeming to peer out from behind a tree four metres or so to their left.

It was second snowman.

"Another…" he pointed, arm trembling.

"Aye, stay alert Jamie." Hector told him as he guided his friend back. "They're all around us, but they do not always move if you look at them, so don't turn your back on them, don't let them creep up on us."

There came the sound of heavy snow falling, and Jamie's head span in that direction, and when he snapped back to the first snowman had gone.

From the dull light came whispers, hushed words spoken in a language similar of Gaelic, coming from all around, then drowned out by more giggling, this time not disguised as children's voices at all, but sounding malevolent and full of malice.

It drifted around the boys and Jamie's breath caught in his throat; tears swelled in his eyes.

"Don't listen tae them Jamie, they'll try tae scare ye, make ye run. We're safer together."

Suddenly they stopped and Hector swore loudly.

"It's covered our tracks."

He swore again, and dread filled Jamie as he stood there shaking, his tear-filled eyes scanning the woodlands. They paused on the closest snowman, which stood just a short distance away, so close that he could see the sharp icy fangs of its teeth.

Another two stood behind it.

"Ah, I think I know where we are." Hector reassured him, and Jamie sniffed and wiped a tear away as his friend guided him back.

To their right another snowman stood its mouth open, eyes narrowed and arms reaching up towards them. From between the trees to their left two other snowmen stood glaring with their black eyes.

Jamie's heart started to race as he saw that there were snowmen all around them.

Hector was pulling him back again, his feet shuffling over snow and foliage, almost tripping a number of times, but Hector held him, guiding him.

Another snowman appeared, cloaked in the darkness that closed in the woodlands and, even as he looked, the snowman's head turned to watch as the boys passed by. A tree branch creaked as it unloaded its snow close by, startling him.

After what seemed like a lifetime, the boys emerged back out into the field. Jamie wanted to collapse, to fall face first into the thick snow that was dazzling in the daylight.

But Hector never released him, taking his gloved hand he

pulled him away, the boys kicking up the thick snow as they hurried side by side away from the woods where three snowmen stood apart, staring out at their retreat.

They did not stop running, not even as a snowball was thrown out at them, followed by another and then another.

They did not stop until they reached the tall wooden gate and hurried through into the safety of Hector's back garden.

*

During the last few hours of that day, the boys played a combat game on Hector's PlayStation, then they each took a long hot bath and had a cup of hot chocolate before going to bed.

Jamie had been wanting to ask his friend about what had happened during the day, but Hector had warned him quietly that they should not speak about it in earshot of his parents.

But, as they lay in their beds that night, Jamie had to talk about the woods and what they had encountered.

"Nae idea what it is, but it's no' really a snowman" Hector explained. "It comes an' goes all year round — where it goes, I dread tae think. It can change its shape, shapeshift into a deer, or a snowman, but it never leaves the woods, that's why naeb'dy is allowed in there alone."

"But WHAT is it? And what does it want?" Jamie asked snuggled up in his warm bed.

Hector sighed.

"Naeb'dy knows Jamie. But it likes tae lure people in. One Christmas it even changed into Father Christmas an' tried to beckon some wee kid in, but they were saved."

"Why does it happen? Why has nobody ever done anything about it?"

67

"Like who?" Hector asked pulling his covers up to his chin. "Wha'd believe there's a shape shifting creature that stalks th' woods? Naeb'dy will. Someone tried affore but it ended bad so we all have to look oot for each other an' stay safe."

"Has it ever tried to take you before?"

"Aye, after we first moved in. Never again. We all keep clear o' the woods an' look out for each other here."

"Has it even taken anyone?"

"Nae, not for years from here. I have heard of hikers disappearing' further north."

"How long has this been happening?"

"Long time Jamie," Hector reported with a yawn. "It knows the woods very well; it talks in Doric which is a very ol' dialect that is hardly ever spoke much these days."

Then in a serious tone, Hector said, "But this is the first time ah've seen so many o' them in one go, an' comin' as far as the edge an' a', it really wanted ye, Jamie."

Jamie had a restless night.

*

He awoke early to the sound of a bird chirping outside and the curtains bright with daylight.

He sat up, yawned and stretched then threw aside his thick covers. Across the room Hector snored deeply, he didn't even stir as Jamie dropped to the floor and made his way between the two beds to the window.

The heating was on but the room was cold, Jamie reached the window and wondered if Hector would be up for sledging. After the events of the day before he didn't really feel like going to the field, even if they kept a safe distance away from the woods like they usually did.

68

Jamie reached up and grasping the curtains, he yanked them open.

The snowman stood right outside the window, peering in at him.

Jamie screamed.

THE END

THE SWING OF THE PENDULUM

Why did we have to go there?

Why didn't we stay away?

Questions that will forever haunt me.

The old house had loomed up over us as we entered through those tall, gothic barred gates. The shadow which loomed down over the three of us was as cold as death. We cycled through those grounds where, over the years, many children had dared each other, seeing how far they could get towards the house before fleeing in terror. Only the brave ones had made it to the stone steps which led up to those huge oak double doors; some had even knocked before turning and running for their lives.

Nobody knew how long the house had been abandoned, the last family to have called it a home moving out many, many years ago. Stories of children disappearing haunted the village, stories of ghosts and horrors passing down through the school halls for generations. The cursed house sat alone on the side of the hill by the woodlands, staring out with its huge wide windows and its pointed slate roofs that towered up above the trees where it overlooked the rolling farmland and the distant haze of the sea.

The grounds were so overgrown that we dismounted our bikes and wheeled them through the wild grass that whispered and grabbed at our legs. I remember glancing up at the highest windows, expecting to see a ghostly face or a shadowy silhouette, but seeing nothing beyond the dusty panes. A shiver ran through me; I felt as if I was being watched.

Deciding it would be best to abandon our bikes, we dropped them to the ground then we hurried across to the house, passing by the old remains of a child's bike that sat rusting away in the grass.

My mind was focused on the stories I had heard, and I hated to admit how afraid I felt. Glancing up I saw birds of prey circling in the blue sky, and there seemed to be a lot of them nesting in the rooftops.

We entered through a side window where the wooden boards had long since been pulled free, and slipping one at a time through the glassless hole minding ourselves as we did so. We found ourselves standing in a huge room with a high ceiling and great double doors that stood ajar. For someone who lived in a council house, I was impressed by the size of this one, single room, and I twirled slowly around staring up at the ceiling that was dull with age, and where cobwebs hung in long, ropy strands. Wallpaper that had faded and dulled was peeling away at the corners and, on the walls, you could see enormous pale squares where paintings had once hung. Mice scurried into the shadowy corners; the place seemed riddled with them.

The house was old and very dusty, we sneezed a countless of times as we slipped out into the main foyer where the marbled floor was thick with grime. A wide staircase with mahogany handrails snaked up to the landing which overlooked the entrance.

And that was where we all saw it.

The huge clock, one of the biggest I had ever seen, stared down from the landing wall to where we all stood. The face must have been the size of a satellite dish, was grey with dust, the roman numeral faded, the gothic hands stuck at 11.03.

The long, brass pendulum with the round disc end, hung

dulled and tangled with strands of cobwebs

I felt a small slither of fear roll down my spine, but unsure as to why. Why would someone leave behind such a great clock?

Alice wanted to go, but Bobby wasn't ready to leave just yet. He was in his glory holding out his mobile and recording the adventure so he could show everyone else at school and become famous. Even the teenagers would give us respect after this.

But it was the stories that unnerved me as we hurried up that wide staircase; stories of children disappearing and curses and ghosts.

We had noticed the mice as we were entering the property. And now there were even more, all lining up along the landing, peering down and twitching their noses at us, small eyes blinking. They did not seem afraid of us, in fact, a number shot across our path as we reached the top, squeaking and snuffling. Bobby went to kick one, and it hurried out of reach before stopping, turning and giving a number of squeaks before hurrying away down the landing. The rest stood silent, watching.

There was a mechanical click and I turned and approached the clock. Bobby wandered away down the corridor on the left while Alice stood there just moaning unhappily to herself.

I did not notice it, not at first.

It was only when I heard another click that I saw that the pendulum was moving.

It had started to swing.

Slowly at first but picking up speed with the momentum. The second hand started to tick noisily as it paced around the face of the clock, showering dust and breaking free from the cobwebs that held it. Mice squeaked and, as if frenzied, started to run in all directions, and Alice started to freak out.

Mystified, we called Bobby but he didn't reply, so we decided to go after him, following his footsteps in the dust, the ticking of the clock following us as we went. Mice crouched in the corners, watching as we peered in every room where Bobby might have gone. We saw a sleeping bag in one room and some clothes, but whoever they belonged to had long since left. More clothing, tatty and torn lay in heaps in other rooms; T-shirts, shoes, trousers, an old cassette Walkman, bags. Even glasses, which peered at us from where they lay, twisted and bent on the floor, cracked lenses sheened with dust.

Alice started to feel faint, maybe it was the dust and humidity of the building; her face looked very flushed and sweaty. I told her to sit down and wait for me, although I really did not want to be on my own.

The corridors seem to stretch out in all directions and I began to feel confused, I started to feel hot and prickly and I pulled the hood of my hoody down. I followed the tracks Bobby had made, calling his name until my voice was hoarse but heard nothing but the clicking of the clock and the sound of mice darting around.

Then, his footprints came to an end in one room. And inside there was yet more clothing.

Bobby's clothes.

I recognised his shirt, and his jeans and his favourite trainers that flashed when he walked. Even some boxershorts that lay crumpled a short distance away must have been his.

A feeling of dread hit me as I approached the clothing and prodded them with the tip of my trainer, moving his tangled shirt aside and revealing his mobile, which stared up at me.

My dread gave way to panic. I backed away, hardly noticing the mouse that watched me from across the room. There were others too, and they started to cautiously approach.

I turned and fled, ramming into the wall in my haste, sweat pouring from me as I ran, shouting for Alice, my hoarse voice echoing around the house while the clock continued to click away.

I ran into the room where I had left Alice and saw her by the window where the daylight seeped in through the boards. She knelt hunched over, her back to me.

"Alice!" urgent, my throat and voice dry. She raised her head and rose unsteadily to her feet. She spoke my name but her voice was low and strange.

She shuffled around turning towards me and I screamed.

Her face was changing, her nose and mouth stretching out to form a snout, her ears, which stuck out from her hair, were large and round; whiskers started to sprout.

She squeaked out my name and held out one hand to me, a hand that had started to twist into a claw.

I backed away, my legs weak, horror clenched tightly in my chest. I crashed into the wall again, screaming as Alice started to stagger towards me, both twisted arms held up and, she too, had started to scream.

I pushed myself away, around and out of the room. My head was spinning, mice squeaking in chorus and the sound of the clock ticked in my head as I half ran and half staggered away down the corridor, swiping away strands of cobwebs that hung from the high, damp-stained ceiling. Ahead the landing opened into the foyer, I saw the clock and that stairs so far ahead. Mice whipped across from the banister posts, squeaking crazily. On the wall the clock ticked and the pendulum swung.

Swoosh, swoosh

The noise of it made my head ache. I was drenched in sweat, burning up, aching. My feet felt heavy, my shoes loose, my tracksuit bottoms hung low from around my waist, and I hastily pulled them up as I hurried towards the stairs. The ticking clock watched as I hurried down as fast as I could, and so did the mice who peered at me, whiskers twitching and eyes blinking.

I was almost at the bottom when I fell.

I hit the marble floor hard with a cry, my body jolted with pain, the burning sensation exploding, my skin prickling like needles. I writhed and cried and clutched at my hoody and managed to tug if off and flung it aside as I quivered and flinched, my sweat drenched body burning with pain and fever, my T-shirt sodden.

And from all around the mice continued to stare.

They watched in silence as I tried to crawl across the floor on my hands that had started to twist and deform, desperate to reach the double doors where the open window waited. One shoe fell off as I slithered and crawled away, but I did not care. I tried to claw away at my T-shirt as I went, slithering across the floor like a snake, but I was unable to do so, and it hung from my body loosely. My breaths turned to pants, tears streamed down my face as I realised that I was unable to crawl or slither any further. My body jolted and twitched.

Mice scurried from the corners, crossing the marble floor and circling around me. They peered down from between the posts on the landing, they watched from the stairs. Noses twitching and eyes blinking, tails swaying just like the pendulum that continued to swing.

And my screams and cries echoed around that old dark house, down those empty corridors, filling the empty rooms and reaching up to its very rafters.

*

The huge house sits in silence.

Dust settled and cobwebs hang.

On the wall at the top of those wide stairs the clock is still, the pendulum hanging unmoving.

Just like time.

From the shadows we do move, scurrying across the floors and through passageways hidden behind the walls.

We watch from the windows, watch the outside world as it moves with time, days going by one by one.

Bobby, Alice and all the others who entered and never left, living our lives in this tortured state, tormented by regret of ever stepping foot inside. Watching and waiting at the dusty windows or from cracks in the door and walls, watching and waiting for those foolish enough to enter this dark, cursed dwelling…and knowing that, really, there is nothing we can do to stop them.

One day someone else will come in, and the pendulum will swing again.

THE END

BEASTLY BEHAVIOUR

Lisa wished that she could like her brother.

She was what her mother called a kind soul; a good natured, caring person who was always helpful to others. She tried to harbour no hatred or ill will to anyone but, sometimes, Joe drove her to her limit.

Lisa and Joe were twins, and were identical only in looks. Personality wise, they were the complete opposite, by miles – galaxies – really.

Joe was nasty, spiteful and very quarrelsome. He was always in trouble at school, never doing his schoolwork and often getting into fights with other children. Lisa pleaded with him to behave, but he took no notice of her. Lisa loved her brother dearly but hated the way he was.

School was a nightmare and sometimes Lisa wished she was in a separate class from her disruptive brother. They were eleven years old and due to attend senior school the following year, and she hoped that they would be placed in different classes then. He often spent time in detention and was, on a few occasions, even suspended. No doubt, he would soon be expelled.

Joe was known to near enough everyone in town for his bad reputation, just like how Lisa was known for her kindness at church and helping out at litter picks.

And then, *that* incident happened.

Poor old Mrs Dudley.

It was a mild spring day and Joe had gone out that Sunday afternoon to meet up with his buddies, who were, to Lisa, just as obnoxious as her brother. She had told him as he left to please behave, and he'd just smirked back at her.

"Give it a rest, would yah," he snapped as he headed out, pulling his favourite cap down over his head.

Lisa saw Robert and Oliver waiting for him outside and they had a football. Later on, that very same football would smash through the window of old Mrs Dudley's house at the end of the cul-de-sac, where Joe and his friends so often enjoyed disturbing the residents with their abusive antics, Mrs Dudley often being their main target.

"I am ashamed and appalled by your behaviour!" their mother had scolded her son later that evening. Joe rested back on the chair on the decking, pretending not to listen as he fiddled with his mobile. "I want you to apologise to that poor woman, at once."

"Never." Joe snorted glancing up at her. "That stupid old bat took my hat! I am never apologising to her and you can't make me."

He spat a string of saliva onto the ground between their feet.

Lisa pulled a face.

GROSS!

And glancing back up at her and their mum, he smirked before returning to his phone.

*

Joe never apologised to old Mrs Dudley, who lived in her ramshackle looking house with what seemed like a hundred cats. The old woman might have been a joke to most of the adults and

79

all of the children in the town, but Lisa liked her and delivered a small shop to her every Saturday.

That Monday, Joe acted like a hero as he recounted how he had kicked the ball in through her front window and had given her a mouthful of abuse when she had staggered out screaming in rage, a number of cats swarming around her feet.

"Stupid old witch," Joe told those who surrounded him amusingly. "So, I told her what for!"

At that moment Mrs Kingsley entered the classroom. The lesson started and Joe was his usual self; answering the teacher back, generally causing trouble and embarrassing Lisa.

But much later she noticed that he had become unnaturally quiet and withdrawn.

After lunch, Mrs Kingsley was running late and Joe would usually have taken the opportunity to be disruptive by drawing crude sketches on the whiteboard or bullying one of the other children. But, instead, he sat at his desk, looking pale and sheened with perspiration.

"Are you ok?" Lisa asked, knowing full well that something was wrong.

"No," he replied with a wheeze, as if breathless. "Burning up and it hurts, my whole—"

He flinched in his chair as if jolted, and Lisa felt a sense of concern chill her bones. She rushed to his side, ignored by the other students who were either waiting patiently or messing around. Then Joe rose from his chair and a jolt of pain sent him sprawling over his desk. Lisa, at first, could not move; she watched as he writhed across his desk, flinching and jolting, his white school shirt damp with sweat.

"You ok mate?" one his friends asked as everyone turned to stare.

Amy Smith, the girl whose plaited hair Joe so often enjoyed yanking, turned in her chair and started to scream.

His back hunched and his white shirt ripped apart as if made from paper. His scream deepened into a monstrous roar which rattled the windows in their frames.

The others went quiet as they watched, at first unsure what was going on. Some rose from their chairs, some even backed away.

Joe stood up straight, his arms raising and fingers curling into claws; the buttons of his shirt shooting across the room as his shirt pulled apart, exposing a widening chest where thick dark hair started to sprout. Drool spurted from his mouth as his teeth grew into fangs, his jaw popped and cracked as it changed shape. He fell across his table, the metal legs bending beneath the weight as his body expanded with muscles and dark hair, his clawed hands raking the desk as he thrusted himself up, the bones in his legs popping and cracking as they altered shape, his trousers tearing apart.

Lisa stood, unmoving, rooted in place by horror as she watched her brother transforming into a raging beast. And even as the other children finally found the will to move, and started to run out of the classroom with screams of terror, Lisa remained where she was, watching as the beast that had once been her brother writhed around on the floor among the shreds that had once been its clothing.

And she knew in the back of her mind that Mrs Dudley was responsible somehow.

She had turned her brother into a beast.

THE END

THE KITTY KATT

She was the smallest kitten from the litter, and not at all liked.

Ignored by her siblings, she sat trembling at the back of the box in the shadows.

She was just like me: small for my age and odd, teased for how I looked and for why my brain was not as bright or as fast as the others. Although I could not help for how I had been born, I was still taunted for my gentle nature and the tears I so easily shed.

But, too me, she was perfect.

My parents suggested another, but her owners were very happy for me to take her away. So I took her home and named her Katt.

A small, gentle ginger and white kitten with the greenest eyes you could ever see, and her purrs were music to my ears.

Each day after the torment I received at the hands of those who so enjoyed causing me misery and harm, she was the one who would make my tears stop and make me smile again.

In time Katt started to meet me at the school gate and accompany me on my walk home. She was not like other cats. She was far too small and thin and, just like me, people often sneered and remarked at her appearance. But we were the same.

Then, one day as we crossed through the alleyway near to home, the bullies swarmed around us, their grins leering down and eyes blazing in delight. Words of cruelty and unkindness spilling from their mouths as they surrounded me; swarming around me, shoving and poking. I feared for my dear Katt, who danced around my ankles in anxiety, but they held me back and away from her as I cried and shrieked. And they laughed as Katt arched her back and hissed angrily at them.

But their laughter faded as Katt started to change before our very eyes. Her ginger and white fur became thicker and darker as her back arched and grew, her paws expanded, and her claws raking the ground as she doubled, then tripled her size, until she was as big as a tiger - if not, bigger.

Her mighty, monstrous shadow rose up across the wall and over where we stood, the bullies all staring with wide eyes and whimpering as she rose before us, towering over us on her two hind legs.

Katt lowered her head, her pretty green eyes narrowed and angry, teeth gleaming, and she hissed, and the sound which rattled thickly from her throat was like a mighty growl which thundered angrily.

She raised the one giant paw and the bullies took off running and screaming in fright, tears streaking their pale faces.

After school, Katt would be there waiting for me at the school gates. The bullies stayed well away, always huddling together in fright, and made the other children laugh at them. Katt and I would always walk home together and never again would I ever have any trouble with them.

Not with my little kitty Katt around.

THE END

POCKETS

Christopher Dane was the last one to return to the changing room after the PE lesson that morning. Most of the class had already changed and had left, a few others still milled around in no great rush. Rick Grime gave him a playful punch in the arm as Chris passed by kicking chunks of dirt from his shoes.

At once Chris saw that his jumper and shirt had fallen from the peg and onto the bench where his bag sat and, glancing up, noticed that the place where his shorts once hung was now empty.

The boy groaned and shook his head. As often was the case during the manic rush of changing back into school uniform, someone had snatched up his shorts by mistake. Something similar had often happened before, when someone had accidently picked up the wrong jumper or shirt.

Chris scanned the row of pegs but saw no other clothing left behind. He wondered who had changed beside him but could not recall.

He glanced down, and through the gap in the wooden bench saw a grey pair of shorts laying scrunched up on the floor.

Hope cascaded through him, and he crouched down and pulled the shorts out from beneath the bench where careless feet had kicked them under. But his relief was short lived as he straightened up and held them out and saw that they were clearly not his. They were baggy and had an elastic waist, whereas Chris had a button-up waist. He glanced inside to read the name label and saw there was none.

The door opened as Rick and a few others exited, leaving only Chris and two others left. And Chris did not really want to hang around. The stories about the changing room being haunted were legendary in the school and even in the town, and although he did not believe such stories, he did not wish to linger alone in such a place.

His tracksuit trousers were caked in mud from rugby, so he did not really want to wear them, and he definitely did not want to borrow clothing from the school office, so he decided to wear the shorts he found and, hopefully, track down the rightful owner.

*

The shorts were a size too large, short on the leg and looked far too baggy but, thankfully, the elastic waist held them in place on him.

"Maybe, they were left over from the class before ours?" Sarah suggested as they sat together for their history class.

"Maybe, but…" He put his hands into the pockets, they were very deep, in fact they seemed…

Mrs Roberts, a tall stick-thin woman, started the lesson, and all murmurs of talk faded to silence. Mrs Roberts shouted a lot, so everyone was always on their best behaviour.

As the teacher paced the front of the class reading text from an exercise book, Chris started to fidget — he had a terrible itch on his leg just above the hem of his shorts. He scratched, then scratched again.

It felt like something crawling along the side of his leg.

"What's the matter?" Sarah whispered out of the side of her mouth.

"Not, too sure, something is…" Chris scooted back in his chair and peered at his leg in time to see a big fluffy, yellow spider crawling out from his shorts. Sarah screamed and leapt to her feet, her eyes wide and wild with fear as she backed against the window. The rest of the students all span around to stare as Mrs Roberts dropped the book she had been reading from.

In a blind panic, Chris leapt to his feet, slapping and brushing at the spider.

"WHAT FOOLISHNESS IS THIS?" Mrs Roberts demanded, marching over to the side of their desk. The others all looked on, some were giggling silently behind cupped hands.

"A spider, but I don't know where it is." Chris told her, glancing around on the floor by his feet. He was unsure where it had come from either, because he was certain there hadn't been any spiders in the shorts when he had put them on.

"Take your seats and enough of this nonsense." The teacher ordered turning away to the others in class. "AND STOP LAUGHING."

All silent giggling ceased; Chris ears rung.

*

The lesson resumed and after Mrs Roberts had finished reading, the students started writing silently in the books. The teacher sat at her desk, her eyes darting across the room at the bowed heads of her class like an owl on a hunt.

But Chris struggled with his writing, for he kept on thinking about that spider. He was not usually scared of insects or spiders, but what troubled him the most was he had never seen a spider like it before.

It had been like a fluffed-up tarantula.

He dropped his pen and, keeping his head low, reached

down under his desk and slipped his hand slowly into the pocket of his shorts. A cold dampness enclosed his fingers as he reached in lower and lower until his entire hand was inside, and the bitty material seemed to open up and he felt around, but it was like his hand had entered into an open void, a bottomless pit.

A tremor of fear drenched his bones as he slipped his hand further and further inside, and he leaned to one side as he reached as far as his elbow.

Suddenly something sticky tangled around his fingers, and Chris hastily withdrew his hand. His fingers were coated in a light blue sticky thread like a cobweb. He glanced down and saw a bright green goo oozing out from his pocket.

He leapt to his feet, startled, his heart pounding. His chair overturned and crashed to the floor.

"WHAT IS GOING ON?" Mrs Roberts demanded angrily leaping up and marching over, her face an unhealthy shade of red.

The other children noticed the green slime that started to trickle out down his shorts, and the braver ones started to scoff.

"WHAT NONSENSE ARE YOU PLAYING AT, MASTER DEAN?" The teacher shrieked, grabbing his shoulder and turning him to face her. "WHAT HAVE YOU GOT IN YOUR POCKET YOUNG—"

An orange bat-like creature suddenly flew out from his pocket, and all heads shot up as it hit the ceiling and started to flap against it. Mrs Roberts released Chris and took a step back, her eyes wide as she watched as the creature fluttered against the ceiling. And then another flew out, then another.

The class started to rise to their feet, watching as more and more of the creatures flew out from the pockets of Chris's shorts and started to swarm across the ceiling, their large orange wings fluttering and tapping. Some started to fly in circles, and all the children backed away.

Mrs Roberts opened her mouth but before she could do or

say a word, one of the orange creatures hit her full in the face. She staggered backwards — the creature had wrapped its wings across her face and was stuck firm.

"It's stuck to her face!" Rick shouted as the teacher backed into the wall and slid down to the floor, her claw-like hands tugging at the creature. A few of the children snatched up their mobile phones and started to film as they circled the flailing teacher.

Sarah started to scream, and soon others were screaming too as, from his right pocket a thick, green tentacle oozed out and started to wave slowly in the air, and then a second tentacle slithered out from his left pocket. Chris backed away holding up his arms, the feel of them brushed against his arm made him feel squirmy, they made squelching noises as they waved about. A yellow spider fell from the hem of his shorts and hit his foot and scurried away across the floor, causing those nearby to jump aside in fright. Another spider dropped out and then another, huge glops of green slime started to drip out.

One of the girls started to cry while another started to scream. Soon other children started to scream too. Then they started to run, fleeing the classroom as their cries echoed down the narrow hall beyond.

And, during all of the turmoil Chris stood shakily on his feet, arms raised and face pale as goblets of slime dripped thickly to the floor and the tentacles waved before him.

*

Someone had pressed the fire alarm and children started to flow out of the building, followed by the adults who were trying to make sense of what was going on. Some of the staff were by now in the classroom with Mrs Roberts, who was screaming hysterically.

"What's going on?" Rick asked Chris, clearly excited as they all followed the flow of kids down the corridors, talk, crying and screams all loud in the air.

"It's these shorts," Chris said, his voice filled with panic. "I think that they…are alive."

"That doesn't make sense," Rick scoffed

"Really, it's true." Sarah came to his defence. "Someone took Chris's shorts, so he took a pair he found in the changing room."

Rick was silent for a second and, as they were passing by one of the doors which led outside, he grabbed Chris's arm and hauled him out from the flow of noisy children and into the school grounds. Sarah quickly hurried out after them and followed the boys around the side of the building.

Even from outside they could all hear the commotion from inside the building as everyone hurried for the designated fire point on the far side of the school.

"Where did you get those shorts from?" Rick asked, rather flustered.

"I found them in the changing room, under the bench." Chris replied with a frown. "Someone took my shorts."

"I took your shorts." Rick announced patting his chest. "I did it as a joke. Your shorts are under the bench where I was changing."

"You idiot!" Sarah snapped.

"It was a joke!" Rick persisted. "I never meant for…this….to happen. Besides, how can it happen anyway? It isn't possible! How can all those…things…come from your pockets?"

"Not too sure, they're so deep it is as if they never end." Chris shoved his hand into the shorts and all the way down as far as his elbow.

He pulled his hand out just in time.

A huge hairy hand, human-like but about twice the size

size of an adult's, suddenly reached out from inside the pocket and snatched at his hand.

All three screamed, startling two nearby pigeons who took flight as the hairy giant hand slipped back inside. Chris, hastily pulled his shorts down, not caring if the others saw him in just his underpants, and kicked his feet free, flinging the shorts against the wall as he did so. The friends all stood together, staring at where the shorts had dropped to the ground, where they lay, still and unmoving.

*

Borrowing Rick's tracksuit leggings, Chris made his way across the empty gym and into the boys changing room. The school was silent once again, most of the staff and students were outside, assembled into lines.

He held the shorts by the waistband as he hurried into the changing room, the smell of old socks and damp towels was strong in the air. In the silence his feet sounded loud and unnerving as he hurried to the bench at the back, his heart hammering in his chest. And there he threw the shorts to the floor and kicked them under the bench, far back where nobody would see them.

Then, snatching up his own shorts from the floor beneath the bench where Rick had been, Chris hurried out and, as the door swung closed behind him, he was sure that he heard the faint sound of fluttering.

THE END

THE UN-LUCKY DIP

It was a square box, roughly five inches each side, wrapped in brown paper and stuck with sticky tape that had started to yellow.

Carla Alexander, ten years old and who had been to the carnival by herself for the first time, had pulled it out of the lucky dip sack at the stall ran by the PTA of St. Mary's Junior School.

She had thought that it was pretty odd, being wrapped in brown paper while all of the other gifts the other children pulled out were neatly wrapped in coloured paper. And it felt light, as if it was just an empty box, so she gave it a gentle shake by her ear until she felt something light inside.

Jude Vincent, her friend from school, suggested she opened it, but she refused and told him that she would do it later at home.

"Well, make sure you let me know what it is!" he grumbled in disappointment.

Carla loved this time of year when the town held its annual carnival. You could always hear it: the music, people and the whooping from the small funfair. Usually, she would spend hours milling around with her mum in the crowd going from stall to stall, looking at gifts or trying her luck on the raffle or tombola before waiting at the curb side for the parade to pass. It was always so much fun.

And this year the carnival was as impressive as ever: gazebos all shapes and sizes, were laid out in lines on either side of the field and along the top edge. The middle of the field was roped off, as that was where performances took place. In the far top right corner by the children's playground a small funfair stood, lights blinking on that hot summer's day with its bouncy castles and high inflatable slides, a slush puppy stand and two huts selling popcorn and candyfloss.

On the other side of the field, behind the row of gazebos, you could find a beer tent for the adults and a St. John Ambulance volunteer by the entrance. The smell and sounds of a sizzling barbeque from the food tent where burgers and sausages cooked and the sharp tang of onions wafted made many mouths water. A vegan food van stood on the field along with a tea tent and two ice cream vans where the queues never seemed to end.

As her mum had to work from home this year, she had wearily allowed Carla and Jude to go by themselves as they lived very close to the field and both children knew never to talk to strangers. Carla was a big girl now and felt important that she was allowed her bit of independence without adult supervision. Carla and Jude had great fun as they went from stall to stall browsing goods and trying their luck on games such as name-the-bear or hooking the duck, where they each won a small gift.

The carnival was as busy as always with crowds of people who hurried from one stall to another with heaped bags swinging. Children walked with either friends or adults, licking dripping ice cream cones or slurping juices from cartons. Dogs of all sizes panted as they walked happily along, and Carla and Jude laughed in delight at one small dog who looked cheerful as it was pushed around in a pram. At a tombola Jude won a leather necklace, which Carla had to help him to clip on, while she won an art set in a raffle, before they each bought a cake at one of the church stalls.

Finally, with their burger and chips, they found a space to sit on the curb to eat as they waited for the parade to arrive. As they ate, they talked about the time when they were eight when they had both taken part in their school's float for the parade. There had been a 'Save the Ocean' theme and Carla remembered how cool and important it had felt sitting on top of the flat top truck dressed as a mermaid and waving at the cheering crowd as they drove slowly along.

The parade was the best thing about the carnival, with crowds of people lining up along the road on either side to watch, cheer and wave as it pass by, led by the mayor and followed closely by the marching band with their shining trumpets and beating drums. And this year the parade was not a let-down, with a full effort being made by those involved. Carla and Jude leapt and cheered, and waved to their friends who were part of the parade. But afterwards, Carla decided it be best to head home. The carnival was getting very busy and it was getting extremely hot.

"Well, don't forget to tell me what you got in the lucky dip?" Jude told her, wincing against the glare of the sun, his face red.

"I won't," she promised, and she left Jude who hurried back into the mass crowd while Carla turned and left.

It did not take her long to get back, she let herself in with her key and made her way to her mum's office to let her know that she was home. But a note on the door informed her that her mum had had to go out and if she and Jude returned before her then they were to call her. Carla text her mum as she hurried upstairs and threw her phone onto her bed as she dropped down onto the floor and emptied her bag of goods.

The brown papered box from the lucky dip tumbled out and lay in the pile. She picked it up in both hands and held it out.

Strange she wondered, what could it be?

Carla began to tear off the paper, and discovered a thick, strong carboard gift box prettily patterned with decorative coloured dots with a matching lid that was held on by more tape. On the top of the lid using a red marker pen someone had written BEWARE.

Curious, Carla started to peel free the tape and swung the lid open. Inside there was a furry ball the size of her clenched fist.

"Yuck!" She squealed with disgust. Disappointment hit her hard as she realised that she had been a victim of someone's horrid joke. She knew that all gifts donated were from parents or local businesses, so someone must have sneaked it in for a laugh.

Suddenly, from her bed her mobile buzzed, startling her. Leaving the box on the floor, she climbed up and hurried to her bed and snatched up her mobile to see that it was a text from Jude. She was just about to text him back when she heard a noise.

She turned back to the floor where the sound had come from, wondering what it had been. It had seemed to have come from that box, which was on her floor where she had left it. As she watched the noise came again, and from the inside, something punched the lid. Her mobile slipped from her hands and fell to the floor by her feet and, at first, Carla was frozen. The lid jumped again, this time with enough force to swing it fully open. Carla, on legs that felt weak and shaky, walked towards the box; resisting the urge to run, she lowered herself to her knees and leaned over to peer inside.

Maybe some cruel and uncaring person had caught a bird and that was what the…

The furry ball rolled itself over and stared up at her with wide-set eyes that were as red as a ripe tomato. Fear clenched at her throat; her mouth opened but no words would form, not even a scream. Never in her life had she seen something like this.

Two clawed arms suddenly sprouted from its side and, before Carla could do anything, the creature leapt up at her. It was so quick and fast that she had no time to move. It struck her on the front of her shoulder, its claws pinching as they dug into her flesh through her shirt, and Carla screamed as she fell down to the floor.

Fixed firmly against her, the creature trembled and an evil chuckle seemed to come from it as it shifted so that it fixed her with its eyes.

Carla screamed again and, with her hands frantically battered at the creature. Its claws dug painfully into her, making her wince, but her hand hit it firmly and her shirt tore as the creature fell to the floor and rolled away. Carla wasted no time in sitting up and scooting herself back away from the creature.

Below its burning red eyes a split began to form, and Carla watched in wide-eyed panic as she saw its broad mouth full of sharp little teeth. Then the creature suddenly shot forward towards her so fast that she did not even have time to blink. It leapt at her and landed on her lap, its clawed arms swinging against her stomach, and Carla cried with pain as she felt them pinching into her flesh, holding itself tightly against her. She felt its putrid warm breath through her shirt, felt it shuddering as it crackled with its low-pitched laughter. The dampness as it opened its mouth to bite…

She was screaming in both rage and fright as she reached out and grabbed the art set that lay in the rubble of the gifts she had won. It was in a small wooden case, and she used it to batter the creature from her, though its claws raked her flesh as it dropped to the floor and she swung her art set at it. But, despite its small size, the creature swung its claw and knocked the case from her hand. It struck the floor, the clips opening and spilling the coloured pencils and paint brushes everywhere. It suddenly shot towards her once more and Carla rolled away. It shot passed her in a hiss of chuckles and struck her chest of draws. With its claws it quickly scrambled up them to the top where there was a pile of her books and drawings. The creature battered the books and they tumbled with a flutter of pages to the floor and her pictures followed next. Her artwork, anime characters and sketches of her favourite singers and actors, followed as the creature lashed out with its claws, shredding a few of the pictures to tatters.

Carla wished for her mum, longing for her, and even called out in her panic for her. And the creature seems to take a great delight in the mischief that it was causing, for its wicked mouth opened wider and it hissed out more laughter. Carla, reached out and grasped a doll that she had bought and threw it at the creature, which caught it in mid-air and, with one vicious swipe, beheaded the doll. It threw the body back at her and giggled again.

In desperation, Clara snatched at other things nearby – a packet of cheese and onion crisps – which the creature tore open, ignoring the crisps that scattered everywhere. Each time the creature just battered or destroyed whatever Carla threw at it. It turned to the wall and knocked off her small, framed mirror, which clattered to the floor along with a framed picture, and, using its claws, started to climb up the wall.

From where she lay, Carla watched it clamber onto her ceiling and inch across overhead. She crawled away in panic as it crossed over above her and then drop down onto her bed.

Carla stared at her open doorway then back to her bed where fluff from her pillow and shreds of her pink duvet sprayed up into the air as the creature caused its mayhem. She turned back to the doorway and took the chance. She flung herself up to her feet and launched herself for the door. The creature must have sensed her movement as, suddenly, it leapt at her as she flung herself past it and struck her back.

Carla staggered and screamed as its claws pinched into her flesh, her legs gave way and she fell to the floor screaming in fright, which made the creature squirm with excitement, taking great delight in her terror. It bit into her back and she flinched and screamed in pain, tears spilled from her eye. Wiggling up onto her knees, Carla grabbed her shirt and pulled off over her head, and the creature came free, its claws digging into the material as Carla swung it around in her hands and wrapped it over the creature, balling it tightly up.

Its laughter turned to a hiss of rage, and Carla held it tightly as she turned towards the box from which it had come. She shoved the creature and her shirt into the box and swung the lid close and pressed the tape tightly down.

Carla did not know how long she sat there for, waiting for the creature to burst out. For a short while it hissed and battered against the sides and the lid, which she held tightly down, crying as she did so and, the creature, wearily, settled down.

On legs that felt shaky and weak, she hurried to the bathroom, where she checked her injuries in the mirror. Thankfully she only had cuts and grazes, even the bite on her stomach was not so bad and had stopped bleeding. She did not cry; she had already cried enough, but she longed for her mum and hoped that she would be home soon. She needed her.

Just as she was slipping on her pyjama top, she heard feet pounding up the stairs and relief flooded through her.

"Mum," she called as she left the bathroom and hurried back to her bedroom.

She froze in her doorway, eyes wide, gripped with terror.

"So, what is the surprise?" Jude asked turning to her, his sun-tanned face beaming. He stood in her bedroom appearing oblivious to the mess.

All his attention was drawn to the box, the box which he now held against his stomach as he peeled away the tape.

"Must be good if you never even bothered to reply to my text."

"JUDE NO!"

She rushed forward arms out-stretched but it was too late. Jude opened the box.

THE END

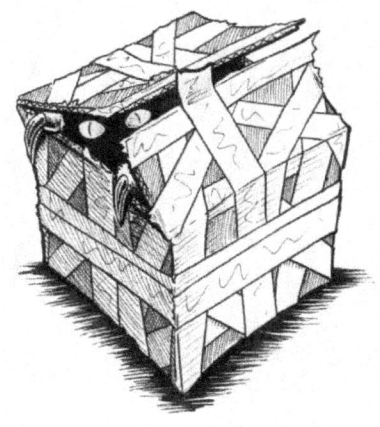

ABOUT THE AUTHOR

Adam D. Searle is a children's author from West Molesey, Surrey, UK.
At the age of 5 he was diagnosed with dyslexia and struggled with his reading, writing and spelling throughout his schooling. He always had a vivid imagination and used tell scary stories to his friends and cousins or make up games. When he was 11-years old, Adam discovered the Goosebump books which helped him to learn how to read and inspired him to become a writer.

Please follow Adam and keep up to date on any new books, projects and events.

www.adamdsearle-author.com